THE KILLER
WORE
A RED HAT

Best wishes
To Bridget & Joe

at Christmastime and
all through the year!

Betty Orlemann

2006

Also by Betty Orlemann

Who Killed Annie?

Sranger In The Woods

Murder On The Canal

Terror In The Shadows

Death Stalks The Wedding

THE
KILLER
WORE
A RED HAT

A Hattie Farwell Mystery

Betty Orlemann

Copyright © 2007 Betty Orlemann

All rights reserved. No part of this publication, except for brief excerpts for purpose of review, may be reproduced, stored in a retrieval system, or transmitted in any form or by any means, electronic, mechanical, photocopying, recording, or otherwise without the prior written permission of the publisher.

This is a work of fiction. Any resemblance of the characters to persons living or dead is purely coincidental.

Cover art by Karen Salee—ksdesign@jps.net

RED ANVIL PRESS
1393 Old Homestead Drive, Second floor
Oakland, Oregon 97462—9506.
E MAIL: editor@elderberrypress.com
TEL/FAX: 541. 459. 6043
www.elderberrypress.com

RED ANVIL books are available from your favorite bookstore, amazon.com, or from our 24 hour order line: 1. 800. 431. 1579

Library of Congress Control Number: 2006938060
Publisher's Catalog—in—Publication Data
The Killer Wore A Red Hat / Betty Orlemann
ISBN-13: 978-1-932762-73-0
ISBN-10: 1932762736
1. Murder—Fiction.
2. Mystery—Fiction.
3. Detective—Fiction.
4. Castles—Fiction.
5. Murder Mystery—Fiction.
I. Title

This book was written, printed and bound in the United States of America.

This book is gratefully dedicated to all of those
brave souls who trusted me to put them in it
Eunha Kim, MD – Psychiatrist, who supplied me with
vital information for this book, and also agreed to be
in it portraying himself.
Heartfelt thanks, too to:
Terri (who also appears in other of my books)
Eileen (who has been in before - Terri's real-life sister).
Six members of The Country Gardeners chapter of the
Red Hat Society who appear for the first time:
Queen Mum Edie, Joyce, Elsie, Kay, Ann and Elaine.
Tinicum Township Police Chief James Sabath,
and once again, Plumstead Township
Police Chief Duane Hasenauer.
And last but not least, Matt Borzio,
Investment Representative.

I just want to add that I thoroughly enjoy putting
live people into my books. It's like casting a play!

chapter one

Through her kitchen window Hattie Farwell could see a brilliant red sky beyond the trees. Anxious to get a better look she went out onto the porch and simply stared at the beauty of a sunset framed by dark green cedar trees. Her giant dog, Wolf, lying in his favorite position at the top of the steps with his great paws hanging over the edge of the porch, wagged his tail in delight when she joined him.

"It's just too bad that you can't appreciate the beauty of this place," she told him with a smile, and he wagged his tail even harder. She never tired of this old farmhouse in which she had been born 81 years ago, and in which her father, grandfather and great-grandfather had been born and lived before her.

Unfortunately, she had been unable to continue running the place as a dairy farm some years ago after the deaths of her parents. She had been forced to sell off her pasture, nearly 100 hundred acres at the top of her lane (a former cow path). Fortunately she could not see from her home the housing development which had grown up there, but when she and Wolf ventured up to see it, she reluctantly admitted that the houses were well built, well spaced and quite authentic reproductions of Victorian architecture.

As to the 100 acres of woods on which her home stood, she was grateful not to have had to sell that or the large wooded area across from her house on the other side of her lane. She had sold the development rights of both properties to the Heritage Conservancy so that the land would remain undeveloped in perpetuity. She sometimes regretted that the option had not been available to her when she sold the former cow pasture. Unfortunately selling development rights was an unknown concept at that time.

Hattie glanced at her wristwatch. It was after 8 o'clock, and the sun was out of sight below the horizon, but its red afterglow remained. She sighed deeply as it began to fade. All at once wolf emitted a low growl. He jumped to his feet and stared down the lane in the direction of the Pike Road. Wolf barked protectively, and Hattie was surprised to see a teenage boy riding his bike toward her house at full tilt.

She assumed that his family had just moved into one of the houses in the development. She wanted to tell him that he was trespassing on private property, but it was growing too dark to send him back to the Pike Road. The boy looked up at the house and for a moment he seemed startled to see Hattie and Wolf.

She waved at him, "Hello," she called, "I guess you are new here."

"SHUT UP YOU OLD BITCH!" he yelled at her and sped by.

For a moment Hattie was nonplussed. Perhaps it was her background as a school- teacher that kept her from running down the porch steps and shoving the rude, foul- mouthed boy right off his bike. She would have to admit that she would have liked to do just that.

However, she did nothing and said nothing. She simply turned and walked back into her kitchen with Wolf at her heels. She flicked the light switch next to the doorframe thus illuminating the hanging lamp over the round oak table. Then she locked and bolted the door.

Her first thought on awaking the next morning was of the teenager and his verbal attack on her. She had been hurt by his unexpected outburst, but she pushed that out of her mind. Maybe, she thought, I was more shocked than really hurt, but what possessed that youngster to yell at me like that? How odd.

As she showered then dressed in her usual attire – black skirt and white blouse, and pulled her gray hair back into a knot at the nape of her neck, she mulled over the mystery. Unfortunately her dear friend, Police Lt. Jim Sawyer and his lovely new wife, Benita, were still away on their honeymoon in Bermuda and weren't expected back for two more days. How she would have loved to tell them all about the teenager and to ask him if he knew of any families who had just moved into the development.

She opened the door at the top of her winding staircase and descended the piecrust steps inside the wall to the kitchen. She tried desperately to remember if she had ever seen the boy before the prior evening. He really didn't look at all familiar to her, but then she hadn't had too good a look at him. "How tall was he?" Jim would ask, "How old was he?" What color were his eyes?" "What color was his hair?"

"Oh, good Heavens!" Hattie said aloud, "I have no answer to any of those questions! He was sitting on his bike. I could only guess his age at about 13 or 14. I couldn't see his eyes and his hair was covered by a baseball cap turned around backwards. And on top of that it was growing dark outside and he was riding past pretty rapidly."

As usual Wolf met her at the bottom of her stairs with happy prancing and vigorous tail wagging. He spun his way to the door which Hattie opened for him immediately. "Be a good boy," she told him with a laugh as he ran outside, "and hurry back for your breakfast." She followed him onto the porch just long enough to pick up the morning paper and return to the kitchen.

She made herself a pot of coffee, scrambled an egg, made toast which she covered with strawberry jam, and read the paper.

Two hours later she saw the mail car stop at her box and hurried out to see who, if anyone had written to her. To her delight, along with bills and advertisements, there was a letter from England from her nephew, Nigel and his wife, Janice.

Having Nigel show up in her life was one of the most wonderful things that had ever happened to her. Her only brother, Fred, had been killed in Europe in World War II, and Hattie always missed him. Once her parents were gone, she thought she was the only one left in the family. What Hattie didn't know was that Fred had married before his death and he and his wife had a son. Fred's wife died in childbirth, and their son, Nigel, was raised in England by her parents, the Stevensons. He knew nothing about his father or Hattie or that his real name was Farwell until his grandfather had died and his grandmother told him about them when she was on her deathbed. As soon as possible after that Nigel went to America and found Hattie.

Hattie tore open his letter with her finger and read it immediately as she stood by her mailbox: "Dearest Auntie Hattie," he wrote, "It has been only two weeks since we were there, and now I believe that we might be returning before you know it! I expect that Walter and Evelyn will be contacting you very soon, but I want to tell you that he is to graduate from Seminary in another week and will soon thereafter be a clergyman. It's a bit more complicated than that, of course, but he's on his way!"

Hattie smiled. She was delighted to think that they might be coming back sometime soon. It was just wonderful to have a family after all these years. Evelyn was Nigel and Janice's daughter and Walter was her husband. Nigel and Janice also had a son, Justin, who was full of fun and reminded Hattie of her brother. And Evelyn looked so much like Hattie when she was young that people remarked on it when the family was visiting.

Hattie carried the letter and the rest of her mail into the kitchen where she placed it on the table. "I'll have to write to Nigel and Janice and Walter and Evelyn, too" she said aloud. Then she looked around. There was no sign of Wolf. Wolf was only a puppy two years ago when someone left him in her woods, and she fell in love with him at once. Her veterinarian told her that he believed the dog was mostly Irish Wolf Hound and maybe one-quarter Timber Wolf. When no one claimed him Hattie kept him. He grew to tremendous size, but fortunately he was sweet and gentle.

"That's strange," she said to herself, "He should have been home for his breakfast long ago." She walked across her lane and down a path in the woods, calling, "Wolf, Here, Wolf come, Come!" but there was no sign of him.

chapter two

The afternoon was drawing to a close, and still no sign of Wolf. In desperation Hattie finally called Plumstead Township Police Headquarters. To her relief the Police Chief answered the phone. He and Jim had been friends for some time, and he had served as best man at Jim and Benita's wedding.

"I'm very sorry to bother you, Duane," Hattie told him, "but Wolf has been missing since early this morning, and it simply isn't like him to go off like this. I've been out in the woods calling him a good part of the day, and there hasn't been any sign of him."

"That's very unlike him, I know, Miss Hattie," said the Chief, "and I can guess how frightened you must be. I'll tell you what, I will be off duty in half an hour and I'll come right over to your house to see if I can help you find Wolf."

Hattie thanked him profusely before she hung up the phone and returned to the woods. Once again she called repeatedly for the dog with no success.

When the Chief arrived, he was accompanied by another

off-duty officer, and they immediately set off on a search for Wolf, each on a different path. Over a fruitless hour later they returned to Hattie's house to discuss their next move.

"Would you care for a cup of tea or coffee while you rest for a moment?" asked Hattie. She gestured toward the round oak kitchen table, and the men sat down while Hattie prepared the coffee.

"Does the dog have any favorite spots?" asked the officer, "Would he be interested in any female dogs?"

"No, no female dogs," Hattie smiled briefly, "He was neutered when he was six months old. I've been scouring my brain all day trying to think of places he might want to visit. I even went into the barn to see if somehow he had been shut in there, but no luck, no dog, just barn cats." With the coffee made, she handed each of the men a fresh mug and passed them cream and sugar.

At that moment the phone rang, and when Hattie answered it was headquarters calling the Chief. "Chief," said the officer when he took the phone, "a man driving up the Pike Road just called on his cell phone to say that he believes there is a body lying next to the road. At first he thought it was a deer, but now he's not sure if it is a person or a large dog which has been struck by a car. It is partially covered by leaves and debris. I've sent out a van." The Chief asked the exact location and with a barely audible "thanks" he signaled the other officer and ran out to his car. Hattie followed them as far as the porch steps, "I'll contact you, Miss Hattie, as soon as we know anything." he said.

The van, with its lights flashing had just reached the site when the Chief and the officer pulled up behind them. It was obvious to them when they left the car and approached the body that it was an animal lying next to the road, and the Chief knew without doubt that it was Wolf.

He knelt by the dog and stroked his fur, "Wolf, Wolf," he said softly, but the dog didn't move. "He's still alive," the Chief said, "but he needs medical care at once." Very gently he ran his hands over the dog, and suddenly stopped in horror, "This was no accident!" he stated, "This dog's legs have been bound with tape!" They carefully lifted wolf into the van and rushed him to the local veterinarian.

The Chief phoned Hattie with the bad news, and she hurried at once to the veterinarian's animal hospital where she joined the Chief and the other officer in the waiting room. The first officers who had responded to the call returned to headquarters. Over an hour later the doctor came out to talk to Hattie and the Chief.

"The dog was bound with tape and badly beaten," he said, "I think it was with a piece of wood or a baseball bat. He has some deep bruises and minor cuts, very little bleeding externally, but I will have to keep him here over night to see what internal damage might have occurred. I'll X-ray him, do blood work and otherwise check him out."

"I wish there was some way to find out who did this to this wonderful dog," the Chief grumbled, "Where is the piece of wood that was used as a club? Maybe we can lift some fingerprints."

Hattie shook her head, "It would be my idea that he was not beaten right out there at the side of the road. It must have been back in the woods somewhere, and I don't suppose that the spot where it happened or the piece of wood will be easily found."

"You're right, of course, Miss Hattie. I just wish we had some clue as to who in the Hell would do such a thing to a wonderful, innocent animal," said the Chief. Hattie took a tissue from her purse and wiped her eyes. She turned to the doctor just as he was leaving the room, "Doctor, may I please see him now?" she asked.

"For only a moment," he said, "Understand, though, that the dog is not conscious."

"Yes," Hattie answered softly, and she followed him into the surgery. The great gray dog lay motionless on the examining table. "Hello, Wolf," she whispered, "You are such a good dog, and I love you. Please get well soon." She patted him very softly and dropped a light kiss on his head before she left the room. Did his tail flip just the tiniest bit? "You go home now, Miss Hattie," said the doctor, "I'll call you if there is any change."

"I'll follow you home, Miss Hattie," the Chief told her, "I would really like to stay with you for a while."

"Thank you very much, Duane," she said, "How about if I make us some supper?" Hattie was relieved when he agreed. "Would you like a grilled cheese sandwich?" she offered when they were in her kitchen, "and coffee?" He agreed to both and she set about making the sandwiches and coffee.

"Something happened last evening which I think I should mention to you," she told him while they ate, "Although it's probably nothing."

"Maybe," he smiled, "but tell me anyhow." And she described the boy on the bike and his unusually nasty remark to her.

"Well!" was all he said, but there was a deep frown on his face.

"Do you know of any new families in the development?" she asked.

"No, not at the moment," he answered hesitantly, "I'll have to look into it."

chapter three

That night before Hattie went to sleep, she knelt by her bed and prayed aloud, "Oh Lord, please help my dear dog, Wolf, and grant that he will soon be returned to full health. Amen."

Despite her fear for the dog she slept peacefully. The next morning she awoke early, as usual. By 5:30 she had showered, dressed, made her bed and was in her kitchen making her breakfast.

She was startled when the phone rang. Even though she was wide awake, it was still very early. Wolf! she thought as she grabbed the phone from its wall bracket. But the call was not from her veterinarian. "Auntie Hattie!" said a man's voice with an English accent, "This is Walter Whyte. I'm terribly sorry if I awakened you. It just dawned on me that you are five hours behind us!"

"Oh, Walter, how good it is to hear your voice! You did not wake me up, I'm a very early riser and delighted to hear from you."

"As my father-in-law told you the other day, I am to

graduate from Seminary next week. As if that weren't exciting enough, Evelyn and I shall be flying over to the States right afterward. Your pastor, the Rev. Arnold Schmidt, told me when we were there that your church is growing so rapidly that they are searching for an assistant pastor, and he has asked me if I will consider the position. Of course, I will have to meet with the members of the Consistory, and the members of the parish will have to approve my appointment, so it's not definite that they will want to hire me, but we'll be there to find out in less than a fortnight. I'll let you know our flight number as soon as I have our tickets."

Hattie was almost too thrilled to speak, "My goodness, Walter, I can hardly believe it. I'm very excited. This is wonderful news. I can't wait to see you and Evelyn." For that brief moment, Hattie's worry about Wolf was pushed from her mind.

However, when the phone rang again two hours later, her gripping fear had returned. This call was from the veterinarian. His first words were comforting, "Miss Hattie, Wolf is much improved this morning, I'm happy to tell you. He will have to stay here a day or two longer just so that I can keep an eye on him, but his injuries are not life threatening. His left front leg is broken. I have put a cast on it. He has two broken ribs and a small crack in his skull. I had to repair a tear in his intestine, but it was not real bad. All in all the dog is very fortunate. He drank water this morning, and I'm going to try him on soft food in a while.

Hattie breathed a deep sigh of relief, "Thank you, thank you, doctor," she said, "How soon can I see him?"

"I'll let you know," the doctor said, "I really want to keep him quiet right now."

"I understand," Hattie said before she hung up. Then she said her grateful thanks to Someone Else.

It was almost dinnertime when the phone rang again. That

time, to Hattie's utter delight, the call was from Jim and Benita. "Miss Hattie!" Jim said in happy tones, "We are home! Our plane just arrived in Philadelphia, and we'll be settling into our apartment real soon."

"How wonderful to hear your voice!" Hattie cried, "And how is Benita?"

"Benita is wonderful! Bermuda was wonderful. Our apartment is wonderful! Everything is just wonderful!"

"Oh, Jim, I've never heard you so enthusiastic about anything," Hattie laughed, "I'm so anxious to see you both. Can you possibly come over for breakfast tomorrow morning? You pick the time."

He left the phone for a moment to consult Benita, and they decided that 8:30 would be fine with them. "I'll see you then. I can hardly wait!" said Hattie.

At 8:30 the following morning Hattie had sausages, bacon and pancake batter ready for the bride and groom when they walked through her porch door – prompt as usual. They rushed to embrace her, obviously just as delighted to see her as she was to have them home again.

After he had hugged and kissed Hattie, Jim looked around, "Where's Wolf?" he asked, "He's always here to greet me." Then Hattie told them the whole story, not only about Wolf's beating but also about the smart aleck boy on the bike.

"That's just horrible!" said Benita, "It makes me want to arrest that boy or something! It makes me want to cry!"

"I know, I know," Hattie said. She put her arm around Benita's waist and led them both to the kitchen table, "Of course there is no proof that the boy had anything to do with Wolf's beating. Come eat, now." They both sat down, and Hattie placed steaming mugs of coffee and the dishes of bacon and sausages on the table. While they helped themselves she grilled the pancakes and then sat down to join them.

After they had finished eating, Jim got up from the table, "It's probably hopeless, but I'm going into the woods to see if I can possibly find the spot where Wolf was bound and beaten. Maybe Duane was right, maybe we can find the club that was used. Who knows?"

chapter four

They all searched through the woods but found no sign of tape or a club. "I'll come back tomorrow," said Jim.

"Don't forget that tomorrow is Sunday," Hattie reminded them, "That is if you want to go to church with me. I certainly don't want to force you."

Jim and Benita both smiled at her, "We told you that we would be going to church after we were married there," Jim stated. "And," Benita added, "I'm really looking forward to hearing Fiona Taylor play the organ again. Is she still living at the parsonage?"

"She is," Hattie answered, "and it seems to be a satisfactory arrangement. She also helps the pastor with such chores as cooking and cleaning in exchange for her room and board. Bertha, her mother has had to return to her housekeeping job at the castle, so Fiona is happy to be busy."

Hattie awoke the following morning to the sound of rain pounding on her roof and windows panes. Thunder grumbled overhead and the rain poured down ever harder. She washed and dressed as usual. She donned a pair of waterproof boots over her shoes and took her yellow umbrella from the stand by the kitchen door.

With no time for an elaborate breakfast, she helped herself to a bowl of dry cereal with milk and a cup of coffee, finishing just in time to rush out to meet Jim and Benita when Jim pulled their car up to her walk, "It's so good of you to come pick me up," she said after the usual "good mornings."

"On a day like this I wouldn't consider anything else," Jim said. "I wouldn't be surprised if we have some flooding. Maybe I'll be called into work." The car splashed through muddy puddles, and they saw that the small tributaries were already topping their banks.

At the church pools of water were forming on the slate path, and more muddy puddles filled the drive. It was impossible to get into the vestibule without getting wet, but fortunately the air was warm.

Not many members of the congregation showed up, but Fiona's organ music was beautiful and the pastor's sermon inspiring. Hattie told him so after the service. He pulled her and Jim and Benita aside until the rest of the congregation had shaken his hand and rushed out into the rain. "I want you to know how impressed I was with Walter Whyte," he said, "I'm anxious to hear him preach and am looking forward to seeing him and his wife in a couple of weeks."

"Thank you Pastor," Hattie said, "I'm looking forward to seeing them again, too."

She wanted to say more but felt it would not be appropriate.

They were about to leave the vestibule when a busty woman of about Hattie's age hurried down the aisle with the altar flowers in her pudgy arms. She pushed right past them. Hattie stared at her for a moment, and then recognition struck her,

"Alice Farnsworth!" she said, "When did you come back? It's been years!"

"Don't make up to me, Hattie Farwell!" Alice Farnsworth screeched at her. You have a lot of explaining to do, and I don't know if I want to hear it!!" With that she charged out into the pouring rain on her way to her car.

"Who was that?" asked Jim in startled tones, "What did she mean? Did you do something to her?" They watched Alice Farnsworth drive rapidly away.

A deep frown furrowed Hattie's brow, "I have no idea what has upset her," she said, Alice and I were never close friends, but she and my best friend, Annie, and I sometimes did things together. "She didn't go to our school. In fact her parents sent her to a boarding school in Virginia so we didn't see too much of her. Then, 50-some years ago or so she married Anthony Farnsworth, rather late in life (or so we thought) and she and her husband moved out West someplace. About a year later she mailed us cards announcing the birth of a daughter. In that day and age she was considered pretty well along to give birth, but as far as I knew everything was just fine. That was the last I ever heard from her, or to be honest even thought about her, so this was a complete shock."

"Where did she live?" asked Benita, "What was her maiden name?"

"Why do you want to know those things?" asked Hattie

"It's just the detective in her," laughed Jim.

"Her family's name was Wellington. They lived in a large walled estate on a hill overlooking our upper pasture. It's rather overgrown now, but it was still beautiful the last time I saw it."

"How about if we drive by there some clear day and have a look," Jim suggested. "I'm curious."

"So am I," Benita chimed in, "In fact I have an idea about

why she is so angry at you. We'll see," she added mysteriously.

"Aren't you going to tell me?" asked Hattie.

"No, not now," Benita teased.

"Hmm," Jim murmured, "You've aroused my curiosity. It isn't raining as hard now, so why don't we drive up there on our way back to Miss Hattie's?"

"That would be fine with me," Hattie said, "How about you, Benita?"

"Oh yes," Benita agreed, "I'm dying to see the place, but it isn't really on the way back, is it?" "Well, sort of," Hattie answered. Benita smiled.

Jim ran out for the car and soon drove to the front of the church to pick them up. When they were settled with their seat belts fastened he started off, "I'm almost certain that I know which way to go," he said, "but maybe you'll want to help with the directions, Miss Hattie."

"Don't drive past my lane," she directed, "but instead drive up the old Toll Road which runs next to my woods about a half-mile before my lane."

They had driven nearly a mile up Toll Road, when Hattie pointed to an overgrown dirt lane to their left. "Turn in here," she said, "This lane was on the edge of my property, but the developer has yet to do anything with it."

Through trees on their left they could see many of the new houses in the development. For a distance of about a quarter of a mile they bounced over water-filed ruts in the road until Hattie suddenly called out, "Stop!"

She pointed to a high ivy covered brick wall to their right. The vines were so thick and the cedar trees next to it so bushy that at first it was difficult to see the wall at all.

Hattie pointed to a slate roof and gabled third floor windows of an obviously large brick house standing a little distance back from the wall. "That's the Wellington house where Alice grew up."

"Wow! said Jim.

"Maybe it's this dark, dreary day, but it looks kind of spooky to me," Benita said, "Do you think that she has moved back into it?"

"Of course I have no way of knowing," Hattie said, "but I guess it's a possibility. Her parents are both dead, of course. She was an only child, and I wouldn't have the vaguest knowledge of the whereabouts of her husband or daughter. After all of these years the house would certainly need a lot of work, wouldn't it?"

"I would definitely think so," Jim agreed.

"Maybe we can find out something about her," said Benita.

"Oh, I don't think it would be right to be snoopy," Hattie said, "I wouldn't like it if it were me."

"Is there any place where we can get a better view of the house?" asked Benita.

"You are snoopy!" Jim teased.

"Why do you think that I became a detective in the first place?" she laughed.

They drove a little farther along the rutted lane until they came to a rusty iron gate hanging on one hinge. It, too, was covered with ivy vines and partially obscured by cedars and wild growth.

Hattie frowned, "As I recall that was the servants' entrance. It does seem very out of the way, doesn't it?"

They climbed from the car oblivious to the softly falling rain. Through the rusted bars of the gate they could see the rear of the house. "It is big, isn't it?" Jim remarked.

"Yes, that it is," Hattie agreed, "I wish there were some way that I could show you the front. It really was a beautiful house as I remember from my youth. I think that we had better leave now. It would be very embarrassing to be caught snooping around here."

chapter five

"It has been decided," Jim said to Hattie when they were back in the car, "That Benita and I are going to take you to New Hope for lunch. Is there any special restaurant that you would like to go to?"

"Any place would be just grand," she said, "Thank you both so much."

The rain gained in intensity to the degree that visibility was nearly obliterated. "With this weather wouldn't it be wiser to go to someplace closer?" Hattie asked. They agreed on an old inn in a quaint tiny hamlet at the end of Toll Road. As they crossed a bridge over a stream which served as a tributary to the Delaware River, they saw that it was already so swollen that it was threatening to top its banks.

During lunch the rain continued to pour down, smashing against the windows and roof. After they had eaten and Jim had paid the bill, they bundled up in their raingear and while Jim dashed out to get the car the women waited for him on the porch.

When he pulled up Hattie raised her bright yellow umbrella, and shared it with Benita. They ran through large puddles to the car. They were not far on their drive back to Hattie's when Jim realized that much of the road was covered with water. He was turning onto a higher road when he spotted a small Toyota stalled at the side of the road they were on. An older woman with a "What-will-I-do-now?" _expression on her face was sitting forlornly in the driver's seat.

Jim jumped from his car to help her, but it appeared that his mission was a lost cause. "Gentleman Jim," said Benita as she watched him get drenched by the downpour. After trying in vain to fix the engine, he shut the hood and opened the Toyota's door and started to help the woman out. Hattie rolled her window down a tad and called to him, "Jim, here is my umbrella. It might help both of you some." She pushed the yellow umbrella out to him.

He quickly ushered the woman to his car and opened the back door so that she could take a seat next to Hattie. "For heaven's sake," Hattie said, "It's Meredith Temple!"

"Hattie!" cried Meredith in real pleasure, "How grateful I am that you and Lt. Sawyer happened along. I didn't know how long I'd be stuck there, and the water is rising."

"Oh, my dear, what an experience," Hattie said, "What were you doing out in this weather all by yourself?"

"Believe it or not, I had come over here for a Red Hat tea at one of the women's homes. As it was most of the women were smart enough not to come, so after I had stayed just long enough for a cup of tea and a tea sandwich to be polite, I started back home. You know the rest," said Meredith.

"Jim and Benita Sawyer, I'd like to introduce an old friend of mine. This is Miss Meredith Temple. We were in school at the same time."

How diplomatic of Hattie to put it that way, Benita thought.

I'll bet that Meredith is a few years older than Hattie. She certainly has more wrinkles. Aloud she asked Meredith, "Tell me about the Red Hat Society. I don't know much about it."

Meredith reached into a large plastic bag in her lap and withdrew a wide-brimmed straw hat in a brilliant shade of red. We all have to be over 50, for starters," she explained, "and of course we all have to have at least one red hat. We also must wear purple – suits, dresses, sweaters, blouses, that kind of thing. It was started in London by a woman named Jennie Joseph who wrote a poem, "When I am an old woman I shall wear a red hat and purple which do not go and do not suit me......" There are hundreds of members in the United States and England, and they belong to chapters of any number of members they wish.

"Each chapter elects a "Queen Mum" who kinds of runs things. The sole purpose of the organization is simply to have a good time. We all dress up in our unusual outfits and go off on bus trips, to teas, luncheons, sightseeing excursions, theatre trips, the choices are limitless. I must say," she laughed, "that we always attract a lot of attention. Photographers seem to love to take our photos for newspapers and magazines. On a recent trip to Historic Philadelphia a woman approached us and asked if we were some kind of religious order!!

"By the way, Hattie, do you still belong to Trinity, the old stone church in Tinicum?"

"Yes, I do," said Hattie, "Why do you ask?"

"Your Pastor, Rev. Arnold Schmidt, has invited us all to church two weeks from today. He says that he will have a "Red Hat Sunday!"

"Well, my goodness, Meredith," said Hattie, "Won't that be colorful?" Hattie believed that would be the day that Walter would be preaching. She wanted to say something, but Meredith had always been a terrible gossip, so she kept her relationship to Walter and Evelyn a secret. She smiled to herself, Arnold Schmidt has always been good at thinking up ways to fill the church, she thought.

Meredith continued, "After church we will all be going to the Sunrise Bed and Breakfast for brunch. They have delicious food there, and I'm looking forward to the entire day. You should join, Hattie."

Meredith lowered her voice and changed the subject, "Hattie, do you know that Alice Wellington Farnsworth is back?"

"Yes," said Hattie, "She was in church this morning." She said no more.

"I bumped into her at the Market on 611," said Meredith, "Yesterday afternoon, as a matter of fact. Hasn't she gotten fat? She used to be an attractive girl, but she's lost her looks now."

"Hmmm," Hattie lied, "I didn't notice. Did she tell you where she will be living?"

"In the old Wellington house as soon as she fixes it up," Meredith was happy to share the news, "Her husband died a couple of years ago she said, and she became homesick for Plumstead Township and her old house."

"You can't blame her for loving that old house. Do you remember how beautiful it was and how lovely the lawns and gardens used to be?" asked Hattie. "Will she be living there alone?"

"Oh, no," said Meredith, "She said her daughter, Jayne, and her grandson will be living with her. As a matter of fact, her grandson was in the store with her. I must say that he struck me as being very rude. Alice was at the deli counter when the boy came up to her. He ordered her to buy a roast beef hoagie with everything on it. No, 'please' or 'thank you' when she handed it to him. Meredith leaned over and placed her hand on Hattie's, "I do believe, Hattie, that Alice is a bit afraid of the boy," she whispered and added, "When I said, 'hello' to him, he ignored me completely. He needs discipline." Meredith drew herself up to her maximum five feet two inches and huffed.

"Oh?" said Hattie, "What does he look like up close?" That has to be the boy, I'm sure, she thought.

"Oh, I couldn't tell," Meredith sighed, "His hair was all over his face, and he was wearing a baseball cap backwards. In addition he had on dark aviator sunglasses. His clothes were black, including black boots and jeans. He was real skinny and not too tall, maybe 5'5" at the most." Hattie said nothing more, but she was convinced now of the identity of the boy on the bike.

Benita couldn't resist probing a little herself, "Is her daughter married?" she asked. "No," answered Meredith in decisive tones, "She's not married and she never was."

"How old is she?" asked Benita.

"She's 49," answered Meredith, who obviously had probed Alice.

"What about the boy?" asked Benita, "How old is he and what is his name?"

Meredith was becoming suspicious of a stranger asking questions about an old friend, "Why do you want to know?" she asked.

Jim poked the side of Benita's leg, and she realized that she had gone too far with her questions. "Oh no reason," she answered innocently.

"That's OK" Meredith told her, reluctant to give up the center of attention, "There's no harm in telling. The boy's name is Ronny and he's 13. Alice told me that they will all be living in the Gardener's Cottage on the estate until the house is ready. All in one breath she continued, "And my house, if you plan to drive me home, is on Old Durham Road in Ottsville. I'll direct you from here."

The rain was still coming down hard when they pulled up her driveway. "Here, Meredith," said Hattie handing Meredith the yellow umbrella once more, "Keep the umbrella as long as you need it."

chapter six

Jim received a call from Headquarters as they drove back toward Hattie's. "I'm afraid that I will have to go back on duty," he sighed, "It looks as though the river is coming over its banks."

"Those poor people who live down there," Hattie said, "They've been through so much already with three previous floods in the past 18 months."

"I know," said Jim, "We'll do everything we can for them." He pulled into her lane which was filled with puddles. When they stopped in front of her house, he looked at it strangely, "Did you leave your kitchen windows open?" he asked.

"Of course I didn't," said Hattie following his gaze, "Something's wrong. I'd never do that." She got out of the car and ran through the pouring rain without benefit of an umbrella.

Jim and Benita followed closely behind. When they were on the kitchen porch they saw that one of the kitchen windows had been smashed. Glass lay all over the windowsill and floor. Hattie produced her key but found the door unlocked. When they went inside they discovered that someone had trashed her kitchen.

In black magic marker a note in childish handwriting had been written on her white wall, "Too bad about your damn big dog!" it said, "I hope you miss him a lot!!"

Hattie stood staring at the note and at her damaged possessions. "Oh Jim and Benita," she said, "I suppose I don't have to guess who did this, do I? At least one thing brings me comfort, he obviously does not know that Wolf didn't die!"

"Don't touch anything, Miss Hattie," Jim cautioned, "I'm going to get a detective and a photographer out here as soon as possible. The flood will have to wait. There are a number of volunteers out there as it is." He immediately put in a call to headquarters.

While they were waiting for the detective and photographer, Jim began filing a report, "Have you had a chance to figure out if anything is missing?" he asked.

Hattie looked around the room again, "No, I don't believe anything is missing from the kitchen, but some of my dishes have been smashed. Would it be OK for me to look into the dining room and living room if I don't touch anything?" she asked him.

"Sure, go ahead," he answered.

"I'll go with you," Benita offered.

"I'll wait here for the others," said Jim. He watched as the women left the room. He felt terrible for Hattie and wanted more than anything to catch the person who had done this to her. She was the closest person to a mother in his life. He loved her dearly and felt protective toward her.

Benita and Hattie walked around the perimeters of both the dining room and living room as well as the center hall onto which both rooms had access. There was no sign that anyone had been in that area at all. The windows were shut tight, but as Hattie remarked, "Since there is a porch around this side of the house, no rain would come in even if the windows had been opened.

"No," Benita agreed, "Do you want to go upstairs?"

Hattie sighed deeply, "Yes, I think I should. This makes me feel so creepy."

"Me too," said Benita.

They climbed the main staircase from the hall and found that nothing had been disturbed in the second floor bedrooms or bath. Even Hattie's room and bath over the kitchen looked normal, "I'm relieved that everything is OK here," she said, "It was just the kitchen which was attacked for some reason…Only the kitchen windows had been opened to let the rain in," she mused, "Why? Why was any of it done? Who hates me so much?"

Her gray and white cat, Cookie, suddenly jumped from her bed and purring rubbed against her leg, "I'm happy to see this cat," she said, bending to stroke his soft fur, "He usually stays in the kitchen. I imagine that when whoever it was smashed the window Cookie hi-tailed it up here."

"I'm glad that he did," Benita said, "He might have been killed if he hadn't"

" You are right, Benita!" Hattie said, "Do you remember when my other cat, Inky, was beaten to death? She picked up the cat and hugged him before she placed him back on her bed. Then she began to look through her drawers and closet, "everything is in order here."

At that moment they heard voices downstairs and went back to the kitchen through the winding staircase from Hattie's room. A woman photographer was just aiming her camera at the graffiti on the wall. A young detective sprinkled fingerprint powder on the table, windowsills, doors, chairs, stove, drawers and china cupboard. "So far there is nothing," he said to Jim, "I would say that our culprit wore gloves. However, there are muddy footprints on the porch," He looked at the photographer, "When you have finished with the mess in here, take some shots of those footprints." He swung his arm toward the door.

After the photographer and detective had departed, Jim and Benita both pitched in to help Hattie clean up the mess. "First I'll see if you have any window glass in your barn," Jim said, "and I'll repair your broken window." He walked out through the rain to the barn to begin his search.

Hattie retrieved her vacuum cleaner, and once shards of broken glass and pottery were swept into a dustpan and discarded, she started to vacuum the floor. Benita tackled the table with a damp cloth, and picked up items that had not been smashed. When Jim returned from the barn, Benita was scrubbing the graffiti from the wall and the room had taken on a semblance of its former self.

"Good!" Hattie said, "you've found window glass."

"When people live in the country they store extras of about everything," Jim smiled.

"Now, Miss Hattie," he said in stern tones, "Benita and I will spend the night here in your house with you. There is to be no argument!"

"Oh Jim is that really necessary?"

"Yep, it is!" he said, unless you want to come to our apartment.

Hattie and Benita both laughed. Their apartment was quite delightful, but Hattie knew that it was small and had only one bedroom. "I don't intend to be a martyr," she said, "To tell you the truth this whole thing is unnerving. I'd feel much better if you would stay."

Jim left them to see what he could do to help out with the flood and resultant evacuation of River Road. "I tried to phone the Sunrise Bed and Breakfast, but there was no answer," she told him as he was leaving.

"I imagine that they left long ago, but I'll try to check on them for you." He said and disappeared through the door.

"I'll just run home and pick up some night clothes and stuff," said Benita, "Come with me, Miss Hattie, we can talk."

While Benita carefully steered her car through the rain soaked roads, they talked about Hattie's nephew, Nigel (Evelyn's father) and his short stay at the Sunrise when he first came to visit. "It's strange how connected we became to the people there during such a short period of time," said Benita.

"Yes indeed," Hattie agreed, "And it's amazing to me how evil those people were whom we believed we knew so well. Leigh and Eileen are the only good people left."

chapter seven

The next morning Hattie awoke at 5 o'clock as usual, and quietly set about washing and dressing before she descended her winding staircase to the kitchen. Oh, how I miss Wolf, she thought as she opened the door at the bottom of the stairs. As she made a pot of coffee she decided to call the veterinarian as soon as he opened and inquire about Wolf. As much as she wanted to have the dog back home she was undecided about asking the vet if he could keep him a little longer because she felt he was in danger.

An hour later the phone rang and to Hattie's delight it was her grandniece, Evelyn, "Auntie Hattie!" she cried, "We will be flying over to the States on Wednesday! Isn't that exciting? Our plane should land in Philadelphia at about 6pm your time."

"Evelyn, I imagine that Benita and Jim (if he isn't on duty), the pastor and I will pick you two up. You are to stay here in my house for as long as you want to. It's a big house, you know, and I would simply love your company."

After the appropriate "thank you" and "I can't wait to see you," they hung up. Hattie had a brighter smile on her face than she had for days. That was the first thing that Benita noticed when she entered the kitchen from the dining room. "Good morning, Miss Hattie," she greeted Hattie, "You are sparkling. What good news have you had?"

Hattie told her that the Whytes would be there in two days. She also told her that very soon she would be calling the veterinarian, "I might ask him to keep Wolf a little longer if he can until we figure out how much danger he is in. But, my, I do miss him so."

"So do I, Miss Hattie. So do I," Benita agreed, "By the way, where do you want to put the Whytes? Jim and I will be moving out anyway as soon as we know that you are safe, so why don't we leave on Wednesday and the Whytes can have our room?"

"Oh, you darling," Hattie said, "You don't know how much I love having you and Jim here. I do know that it has been a bit of a sacrifice for you. I'm certain that you are both anxious to get settled in your own apartment"

"Yes, we are," Benita admitted, "but it will wait. I wouldn't have an easy moment leaving you here alone. Anyway, I'll help you fix up their room on Wednesday and then we can all go down to the airport to meet them in the evening. I'm truly looking forward to seeing the Whytes again. If Walter gets the job at the church and they stay here, I'm sure that we will all be good friends."

"I'm certain of it," Hattie agreed.

At that moment they heard the sound of boots pounding on the porch floor. "Oh good," said Benita, "Jim's back!" And in a few minutes Jim, who had shed his boots, strode into the kitchen in his stocking feet. "Coffee, coffee," he groaned, "before I fall asleep!" He collapsed into a chair at the table and put his head down on his arms.

"Don't fall asleep!" said Benita in a loud voice. "Here's your coffee." She slid a full mug in front of him.

"How bad is the flood?" Hattie asked him.

"Real bad," he sighed, "River Road is closed for almost its entire length. People have had to be evacuated from the homes along the river. Many of them have flooded first floors."

"Have you heard anything about the Sunrise Bed and Breakfast?" asked Hattie with a concerned frown. "Leigh Wall put so much time and money into fixing it up when she took it over after all of the troubles. I hope that nothing happened to it."

"The canal is between the Sunrise and the Delaware River," Jim reminded her, "And the inn does sit up quite high. Anyway, think about this, it's an old Victorian house, and I'll bet that it has survived many floods in its lifetime."

"Yes." said Hattie doubtfully. A worried frown furrowed her brow.

Outside the rain continued to pound on the porch roof.

At mid-morning Hattie put in her call to the veterinarian. "Wolf gets better every day," he told her, "But I'm certain that he really misses you. He's well enough for you to pick him up this afternoon when I can fill you in on all of his care. I'm sorry to seem to be rushing him out, Miss Hattie, but we've been invited to visit some relatives in Michigan, and we really want to go tonight."

Hattie hesitated for a moment before she said, "I'll be there. You and your wife just go on to Michigan and have a wonderful time. What time shall I come?" Benita cocked her head and looked at Hattie with a frown. When Hattie and the veterinarian had terminated their conversation and Hattie had hung up the phone, she turned to Benita, "The veterinarian is going away, so Wolf will be coming home today. I'm sure that I can care for him, and you folks will be here to help if necessary."

"You are so right, Miss Hattie," she said. She turned to look at Jim who was just finishing his second cup of coffee, "You should go right up to bed," she told him, "You look awful!"

He laughed, "Yes ma'm," he quipped. He pushed himself away from the table slowly and made his way through the dining room to the hall and up the stairs.

chapter eight

Wolf could hardly contain himself when he saw Hattie at the veterinarian's that afternoon. He cried and rushed to her as fast as his injuries would permit. She surprised herself by crying when she hugged him and kissed the top of his head. With her arms still around the great dog, she turned to the smiling doctor, "He's really going to be fine, isn't he?"

"Yes, he will recover fully if you follow my instructions, and I'm sure that you will. Keep a close eye on his broken leg, and don't let him walk on it any more than necessary. If it should become swollen and hot call me at once. Keep his diet relatively bland, but give him as much to eat as he wants, and make sure he gets plenty of water," He handed Hattie a packet of pills, "These are antibiotics," he told her, "Make sure that he gets one a day. That's about it. I'm sure he will be fine – especially now that he will be home with you. Oh, one more thing, take him out on a leash only to perform his duty, and do not permit him to run free."

"You can trust me, Doctor," Hattie said with a smile, "I'll treat him like a baby." "A mighty big baby," laughed the doctor.

He handed her the list of instructions he
had just given to her verbally, "Call me any time if you have any problems, and if you need emergency care while I'm away, here's the name and number of a veterinarian on 413." He gave her a card.

Hattie thanked him heartily and left. Wolf had a little struggle climbing into the back of her station wagon, but once in he circled as he always had and lay down on the blanket she had provided for him. Before she turned on the ignition she looked back at him, and he wagged his tail happily. "I really love you," she told the dog, and he wagged his tail even harder.

By Wednesday he was well enough to leave the kitchen and take brief walks outside with Hattie . He did not attempt to climb the stairs to the second floor, yet, but Hattie assumed that he would not until his cast had been removed.

Cookie, the cat, had greeted him as warmly as anybody had, and when Wolf went to his bed beside the fireplace, Cookie, purring loudly, curled up next to him and slept.

At lunchtime Benita and Hattie sat at the kitchen table eating sandwiches. Jim came in while they were eating and joined them, and then Wolf and Cookie both went to them and begged for scraps. "Just like old times," Jim chuckled, "But no scraps this time. I'm sorry, but you have to get well first." Wolf put his head on the edge of the table and rolled his eyes up to Jim beseechingly. "Sorry, old man," Jim laughed.

"Jim," Hattie said, "One thing worries me, we will be leaving for the airport at about 4 o'clock and we won't be home until 8 or 9 this evening. What if someone breaks in again during that four or five hours? What if they attack Wolf again and maybe even Cookie?"

"I thought about that possibility," Jim said, "So I've arranged for one of our men to stay here while we're gone. Everything should be fine." Hattie breathed a sigh of relief.

Jim went around the house and checked all of the locks on the doors and windows. At 3:45 the pastor arrived followed closely by Officer Don Dolan. Jim filled the officer in on the recent attack against the dog and break-in of Hattie's house. "I've heard about both of those things, Lieutenant," he said, "And believe me I'll be on my toes."

With thanks to Officer Dolan and pats on Wolf's head, Jim, Benita, the pastor and Hattie left for the airport at exactly 4 PM.

chapter nine

"Benita," Hattie said during their ride to the airport, "You did a wonderful job cleaning the bedroom and bathroom for Evelyn and Walter. Thank you very much. They should feel at home, I'm certain. Now, have you finished packing for your trip home to your apartment?"

"Oh, heavens, yes," laughed Benita, "there was really very little to do. In fact, I put everything into the back of this van when it was parked out next to your house."

Hattie was grateful for the parking area she had designed between her house and barn. It was very convenient for her as well as her guests.

The traffic in the Philadelphia Airport was thick as usual, but Jim found the Overseas Terminal less busy than the domestic ones. He dropped Hattie, Benita and Pastor Schmidt off in front of the terminal and drove to the adjacent parking garage where he had no trouble finding a parking place.

The plane landed at precisely 6 PM, according to the board, and within 15 minutes Evelyn and Walter hurried out to greet them and find their luggage on the carousel. Hattie embraced them warmly and they returned her hugs and kisses lovingly.

Although she didn't say so aloud, Hattie was filled with gratitude once again for a real family. After all of these years I finally have a real family again, she thought. The seven passenger van, with its six passengers, was filled with happy chatter all of the way back to Hattie's house.

You are to have the same bedroom you had the last time you were here. The big corner room at the back of the second floor.

"Oh," Evelyn said with pleasure, "I'm so glad. That's a very comfortable room with a lovely view of the woods."

Benita and Hattie shared a knowing smile but said nothing.

In the meantime at Hattie's house, Officer Dolan heard a strange sound coming from the lane. Wolf uttered a low ferocious growl. The officer managed to open the porch door a crack and squeeze through the opening without letting Wolf push his way out.

As he told the story later, he saw a shadowy figure prowling around Hattie's, the pastor's and his own cars. The figure, which appeared to be thin and not too tall, was apparently holding a baseball bat in his right hand. "Hey there!" Dolan said he yelled, "What are you doing out there?" He started down the porch steps with his gun and flashlight both held in his right hand. The figure suddenly flung the bat at the officer taking him off guard as he drew close. The bat struck Dolan hard on his right shoulder. The gun discharged harmlessly and, with the flashlight, dropped to the ground. The boy straddled his bike and rode rapidly up Hattie's lane, Dolan recounted.

Officer Dolan held his arm against his body. The pain was excruciating, and that's how Jim and Hattie and the others found him not more than five minutes later when they drove up the lane. After he had told his story when they were waiting for an ambulance, Jim asked him, "Don, how well did you see this person?"

"Not well," answered Dolan, "He was pretty much in the shadows."

"What was he wearing?" Jim asked.

Dolan hugged his right arm closer to his body and grimaced in pain, "Dark clothing. What appeared to be a black shirt, dark pants and a baseball cap turned around backwards."

"How old would you say he was?" asked Jim.

"Because of his build and his clothing I would guess him to be young," Dolan answered, "Maybe 13 or 14 at the most," he paused for a moment and then continued, "Two good things, though, he didn't take the time to pick up his baseball bat, and he didn't smash it into the cars. I'm certain that was his intent. Also, he didn't seem to realize that Wolf was inside the house."

"Thank Heaven for that!" Hattie said.

At that moment the ambulance arrived. Dolan had the presence of mind to hand Jim his car keys before he was driven off, "You know, I could have gone to the hospital in a car," he said. Jim picked up the gun and emptied it. He just shook his head as the ambulance left. Then he picked up the baseball bat very carefully with his handkerchief in order to take it back to headquarters for DNA and fingerprint testing.

chapter ten

Walter spent much of the rest of the week with the pastor or writing his sermon for Sunday's service while Hattie and Evelyn got to know one another much better. For Hattie looking at Evelyn was almost like looking at herself in the mirror nearly 60 years before. "Our resemblance is uncanny," she said one day, "You could be my granddaughter."

"After all of these years," Evelyn said with a smile, "You are everything to me that a grandmother should be." Hattie got up from her chair and hugged Evelyn. Her eyes brimmed with happy tears.

"Excuse me for a moment, dear," Hattie said dabbing at her eyes with a tissue, "I've been trying to reach someone at the Sunrise Bed and Breakfast. I've been very concerned about them since the flood." Once again she dialed the number, and this time to her delight Eileen answered the phone.

After the usual happy greetings Eileen told Hattie that the flood waters, though on the property never reached the inn itself, "Everything has been drying out for the last several days, and it's getting to look almost like normal around here. I'm sorry that we weren't here to get your call, but as you probably know we were evacuated. Another good thing is that the well water was not contaminated. So we're in business!"

"I'm so glad," said Hattie, "and especially happy that you and Leigh are fine. An old friend of mine is a member of the Red Hat Society, and she has invited me to come to their brunch at the Sunrise on Sunday after church, so I'll see you then."

Eileen told Hattie that she was delighted, and when Hattie hung up the phone she had a wide smile on her face.

"I love that girl," she told Evelyn, "Leigh Wall, the owner, and the previous co-owner hired her some time ago to work part time to help in any way they needed. The other owner is gone now, I'll tell you all about that some other time if your father hasn't told you already.

"Anyway, Eileen was a flight attendant before she married a pilot and then had two little boys. She gave up that work in order to stay home with the children as much as possible. You must meet her. Maybe you can come with us to the brunch on Sunday."

"That sounds like fun, Auntie Hattie, but would they want someone my age?"

"I believe that you would be most welcome. I don't believe they are prejudiced against young people! Maybe we can sit at another table, anyway. After all I'm not a member either and I don't have a red hat!" They both laughed.

chapter eleven

Evelyn was visibly nervous as she dressed for church on Sunday. Walter, on the other hand was calm and cheerful.

"This heat is something we are not often used to in England," he said to Hattie when they were all in the kitchen. He ran a finger around the inside of his Roman collar. "Will it be hot in church?" he asked.

"I doubt it," Hattie answered, "I can't say that I remember it ever being very hot. Those wide stone walls are very efficient at keeping out the heat."

"Will this dress be all right?" Evelyn asked, "what do the women usually wear?"

Hattie looked with approval at Evelyn's light blue skirt and matching blouse. The skirt fell to a spot just below her knees. "Evelyn, you look lovely. Your outfit is perfect. As to what the women wear, they all wear just what they want to. Some wear long skirts, some wear blouses and pants, and some wear skirts the length of yours. Some wear pumps like yours and some wear sandals. You look just fine, so now forget yourself!"

Walter laughed, "A fine recommendation, Auntie," he said, "Now let's go to church."

As Hattie drove her car she stole an admiring glance at Walter from time to time. He looks very handsome in his clerical attire, she thought. I hope the congregation will like him.

As soon as Hattie parked the car, Walter hurried into the sacristy to join Pastor Schmidt. Evelyn and Hattie with time to spare strolled through the cemetery. As she did each week Hattie paused at the graves of her parents and brother, Fred, and at Annie's grave, too. She was pleased to see that they were well kept as usual.

Evelyn stared at Fred's gravestone. "The grandfather whom I never met," she said wistfully. At that moment the church bell began to toll.

Hattie looked at her wristwatch, " Ten-twenty," she announced, "We have ten minutes until the service starts. We'd better go in, look at all of those people!"

They joined the crowd going through the door. The greeters handed them their church bulletins and smiled warmly as they said, "good morning" to everyone.

A large section of pews on the left side of the church had been reserved for the Red Hats and they were filling them rapidly. "Does Walter know about this being RED HAT SUNDAY?" asked Hattie.

"Yes, I believe he does," said Evelyn, "He wouldn't tell me what subject he has chosen to preach about. I wonder if he will include the Red Hats." She felt nervous again.

Benita and Jim climbed over a couple sitting on the aisle and sat next to Evelyn. Hattie leaned across her and patted their hands, "Good morning," she whispered.

"I have an officer assigned to drive by your house every fifteen minutes or so," Jim whispered back. Hattie sighed with relief.

The organ, which had been playing softly while an acolyte lit the altar candles, suddenly burst into the opening hymn, and the congregation rose to sing. A crucifer led the way down the aisle followed by the choir, servers and Walter. Pastor Schmidt brought up the rear. "This is most impressive," whispered Evelyn.

The pastor stood in front of the congregation with Walter at his side. They gazed down at a sea of red hats, and they both laughed. The ladies in the red hats laughed with them at first and were soon joined by the entire congregation.

"Some of you will remember the Rev. Walter Whyte," said the Pastor, "He took part in a recent wedding ceremony." He looked pointedly at Benita and Jim. Everyone smiled, "only," the pastor continued, "he was still just finishing up in seminary at that time. Now he is an ordained minister!" The congregation clapped. "Walter is here from England with his lovely wife, Evelyn. Stand up, Evelyn," She did so to applause which she graciously acknowledged. "Walter will preach today's sermon," the pastor finished.

Evelyn tried to pay attention to the prayers and scripture reading, but she was so anxious about Walter's sermon that they didn't sink in too well. Finally the time had come. Pastor Schmidt accompanied Walter to the pulpit and watched him as he ascended the two steps. Walter placed some notes on a hidden shelf, put his hands on the pulpit's sides, and with calm self assurance leaned forward and smiled at the congregation.

"Good morning," his clear bass voice rang out through the church, "I wish I could tell you how much it means to me to be back here at Trinity with all of you." He glanced down at Hattie and saw that she was beaming with pride. To his relief he also noticed that Evelyn had finally relaxed. She too smiled up at him as did Jim and Benita.

"As you know, I am from England, but I will try very hard

not to be too English. Please, if you cannot understand what I say because of my accent, raise your hands. I've worked too hard on this sermon not to be understood!" the congregation laughed.

But Walter was understood and appreciated.

"That was one of the best sermons I have ever heard," Meredith gushed after the service. Somehow she had pushed herself to the front of the line leaving the church, and was the first to shake Walter's hand, "I just had to be the first to shake your hand!" Walter smiled at her in appreciation when he took her hand in his, "Thank you so much for your kind words." he said, and added sincerely, "That is a lovely red hat."

She thanked him and seemed about to say more when Hattie came up behind her, greeted her warmly and with her arm in Meredith's walked her out of the church and down to the walk. "Meredith," Hattie said honestly, "You really look lovely in your purple pants suit and red hat."

"Thank you Hattie," said Meredith, "Look, here comes our Queen Mum Edie Rapp with Joyce Houston, Elsie Wood and Kay Smith. They are all members of this church, aren't they?"

Hattie turned and followed Meredith's gaze toward the church as the four women approached. "Yes, said Hattie, and they are all friends of mine, too. They certainly look fine in their purple outfits and red hats, too, don't you think?"

More and more women in like outfits filled the walk and the driveway. Two more ladies in their red hat outfits came up to Hattie, "Hattie," said one, "do you remember me? We once taught school together for a short time in Easton."

"Of course I do," Hattie said, "You are Elaine Anderson, and you haven't changed a bit. It's so good to see you again."

"Thank you Hattie, neither have you," Elaine drew another woman forward, "This is Ann Herbsleb, Hattie, she moved in not too far from here a year ago. Ann grew up in England and really appreciated Walter Whyte's sermon."

Hattie greeted Ann warmly, but before she continued conversing, she turned to make sure that Evelyn was all right and saw that she and Benita were enjoying an animated conversation. "Hattie," said Queen Mum Edie, "We've been discussing you and think it would be wonderful if you would join our chapter of the Red Hats. We've named it "Country Gardeners."

"Oh, please Hattie," Joyce begged her, "We have such good times and you would be a welcome addition." "Yes Hattie, please," the others joined in.

"Well," Hattie began hesitantly, "I'm not too good a gardener."

"Most of us aren't," laughed Kay. "We would just love to have you as a member," added Elsie. "You don't have to be a gardener at all,"

"I don't think that I have the proper attire," Hattie lamented, "but, of course, if I join, the first thing I'll buy will be a red hat!"

"Of course!" Meredith stated, "And Hattie, that beautiful purple dress you wore to Jim and Benita's wedding would be perfect!"

"Don't you think it's too dressy?" Hattie asked.

"No," they all said at once.

"After a while you can buy a purple suit or something, but that dress is gorgeous!" Edie said, "And by the way, we meet only once a month, and we don't do anything else but have fun!"

Hattie laughed, "How can I resist? Anyway it should be fun to just pal around again with my old friends. Thank you everybody, maybe it's time for me to let down my hair! I accept."

"Good!" they all exclaimed, "And now," said Edie, "We'd better get down to the Sunrise for our brunch. I see a bunch of the others have left already."

Hattie turned to find Evelyn who was just hurrying down the path toward her, "Auntie Hattie," she said, "Pastor Schmidt has invited Walter and me to have lunch with him and the members of Consistory. Fortunately he was able to round them up as they all came to church this morning to hear Walter preach. I'm sorry, but of course I shan't be able to go to the brunch with you."

"Don't even think about that, Evelyn," Hattie said, "There will be many other times for us to have brunch, and this sounds much more exciting." She handed her car keys to Evelyn, "Here take my car wherever you are going. I'll get a ride home with one of my friends. And if for some reason I'm late you'll find a kitchen door key under a flower pot at the back of the porch."

Evelyn took the keys, "Thank you ever so. I too hope lunch will be exciting, Auntie, I do hope so," Evelyn answered, "It is rather nerve racking, though." Almost as an afterthought she added, "I hope you will enjoy your brunch, too."

chapter twelve

When Hattie and her friends were walking into the Sunrise, Hattie asked Edie, "Are all of these women members of 'The Country Gardeners'?"

"No, some are from other chapters. I have seen most of them many other times, though," Edie said. She looked around and stopped walking when she spied one woman striding alone up the path. The woman was tall and thin and appeared to be young, but she wore the brim of her red hat so low that it was impossible to make out her features. She wore a purple pants suit and red pumps with spike heels which were at least three inches high. "Now there is a complete stranger to me," she said. She turned to her group of friends, "Does any of you know who that woman is?" she asked nodding her head in the direction of the stranger.

The others glanced at the stranger, but no one recognized her. "I guess that she's new, but why aren't any of the others in her chapter with her?" asked Meredith, "By the way, does anyone know if Alice Wellington Farnsworth was in church this morning?"

"I didn't see her," said Hattie. Nor did anyone else.

Hattie smiled to herself when Meredith hurried into the dining room ahead of all the others and seated herself at the side of a long and elaborately decorated table. Turning quickly she beckoned to Hattie to sit in the chair next to her. Hattie looked around and saw that all the table clothes were red and the napkins purple. The centerpieces were filled with red geraniums and purple iris, "Beautiful," she said aloud as she sat down.

Suddenly someone placed her hand on Hattie's arm and she turned to see Eileen's blue eyes looking down at her. Eileen, only five feet tall and pretty as a picture, was smiling broadly, "Miss Hattie!" she exclaimed, "You look wonderful, and I am so happy to see you."

Hattie rose from her seat and took the young woman into her arms, "And Eileen, I am so happy to see you, too. I've been looking forward to this for some time. And you look wonderful, yourself!" She introduced the young woman to Meredith and some of her other friends before she had to rush off into the kitchen., her dark brown pony tail bouncing behind her head.

Meredith had no lack of things to talk about during their meal. She was particularly interested in the other ladies and told Hattie little stories about everyone whom she recognized. At one point she gazed at the slender stranger who was sitting two tables away. "She seems to have made friends with some of the others," Meredith observed. Hattie glanced over at the newcomer who was listening carefully to some of the women who were talking to her.

"Hattie," said Meredith, "There is something familiar about that woman, but with her hat pulled down over her eyes that way it's hard to tell what she looks like."

Elaine, Elsie, Joyce and Edie all took their cameras and

went from table to table taking pictures of everyone. It was an innocent endeavor, Hattie realized, and probably something they did at every meeting. Others were doing the same. The thin stranger two tables away apparently did not want to be in a picture. She pulled her hat even farther down over her eyes and turned away every time she saw a camera coming in her direction.

A loud rumble and a flash of lightening announced the approach of a thunder storm. "Not another one," Elsie groaned. But another one it was and a loud and furious one with high winds and pouring rain.

Eileen with Leigh Wall's help had just finished serving the desserts when all of the lights went out. Hattie picked up a pack of matches from the table and lit the two candles in the centerpiece. Others soon followed her example, because even though it was mid-day it had grown quite dark.

Leigh Wall came over to Hattie's table and greeted her effusively. Hattie introduced her to the others, "This is the owner of the Sunrise," she said, "and an old acquaintance of mine. How have you been, Leigh? You look wonderful."

"I guess that widowhood agrees with me," Leigh responded with a little chuckle.

"That remark deserves an explanation," Meredith whispered in Hattie's ear.

"Later," Hattie answered softly. She tried desperately to think of some way to change the subject. Leigh's husband had been murdered almost two years ago and his body had been found in the canal. That was certainly nothing she wanted to talk about now, and especially to Meredith.

Suddenly Meredith with Leigh forgotten rose rapidly from her chair. She stared at an empty place two tables away which had been occupied by the mysterious woman, "She's gone!" she said.

"For goodness sake, Meredith," said Elaine, "Maybe she just went to the ladies room."

"I'll go look," said Meredith. And she hurried from the room.

chapter thirteen

Ten minutes passed and neither Meredith nor the thin stranger returned, "Now what could have happened to Meredith?" asked Edie, "She should have been back before this."

Eileen, who was passing the table just then said, "I saw her going outside shortly after she left the dining room. It was still raining and she was carrying a yellow umbrella."

"That was my umbrella," said Hattie, "I had lent it to her. I can't imagine where she would be going in the rain. Anyway, she had said she would drive me home, so she couldn't have gone too far."

"Oh well, she'll be back soon, I'm sure," said Joyce cheerfully, "And if not, Hattie, I'll drive you home, don't worry."

Hattie laughed, "thank you Joyce. I'm really not that concerned."

"Would you ladies like to have coffee or tea in the parlor?" Eileen asked as they started to leave the dining room. When they all accepted she led them to a cozy sitting room in the front of the house overlooking the canal and river. There they sat and sipped their drinks, and while nibbling on tiny breakfast cakes they made their plans for their next meetings.

"You all were right about the Red Hats being fun," said Hattie, "I don't remember when I have been more relaxed." However, she was not to be relaxed much longer.

"My gosh!" Kay said suddenly, "Will you look at the time? It's after four o'clock!"

As if on command every woman in the room looked at her wrist watch. "Where is Meredith?" said Hattie, "There is no conceivable reason for her to be gone this long, and especially in the rain!"

Eileen came into the room to take the cups and saucers back to the kitchen, "Isn't your friend back yet?" she asked when she was loading her tray.

"No", said Elsie, "And to tell you the truth we're getting worried about her."

"That is strange," Eileen said, "It must be close to two hours since I saw her walking some distance behind that other lady. And it's still raining."

"Why would Meredith go out walking in the rain at all, much less for all of this time?" Joyce mused.

"Well, rain or no rain, I think that we should go out and look for her," Hattie said.

Some of the women had gone home, and a few of the others were preparing to leave, but Edie, Joyce, Elaine, Ann, Elsie and Kay all volunteered to go look for Meredith. "Maybe she fell and hurt herself, "Elsie said. We can't just leave her here."

Eileen pointed out the path that she had seen Meredith taking. She stood on the porch outside the front door with them while they finished fastening their raincoats and raising their umbrellas, "She was on that path right there. The one that runs next to the canal. She couldn't have gone too far on that, because some of it was washed out in the flood. The only thing that I believe she could have done is take the bridge over the canal and follow the path along the river, beyond the towpath on the other side."

"The river is still moving rapidly, isn't it?" said Edie.

"And look how brown it is. Not quiet and pretty the way it usually is." Said Joyce.

"It sort of gives me chills," Kay joined in.

The women walked together down the path and over the canal bridge, past the towpath to the narrow path along the river that Eileen had told them about. With Hattie and Edie walking rapidly in the lead they hurried along that path.

"I'm going to take my hat back to my car," Elsie said, "I don't want the rain to ruin it. Does anyone else want me to take their hat?"

With that they all took off their hats, "I'll go with you, Elsie," said Kay. We'll be right back." With all of the hats protected by their umbrellas they hurried back to the parking lot.

The others continued along the river path.

Suddenly Hattie stopped, "Look, over there in the bushes. I see something bright yellow, and I'm afraid it's my umbrella!" She pushed the bushes aside and struggled through high growth and mud down the river bank, "It is my umbrella," she called up to the others, "It's open and upside down, but there is no sign of Meredith."

"Maybe we had better leave it there," said Edie, "If we don't find her soon I think we should call the police."

Hattie looked around but saw no sign of a struggle. "Maybe it blew out of her hand," she said doubtfully, "Let's go on down the path."

"Slow down a little," said Elaine about 15 paces later, "Maybe we are missing something."

At that moment Ann cried out, "Look over there floating

on the river! It's a red hat!" The others gathered around her and looked at the spot where she was pointing.

"Oh, it is a red hat!" said Elaine. The hat was washing in and out on the waves at the water's edge.

"Oh-my-gosh!" said Edie, "It really looks like Meredith's hat!"

"But where is Meredith?" said Hattie. Her question was answered at that moment by a horrified scream.

They all turned around to see Elsie and Kay who had been hurrying to join them. They were standing frozen in place staring down into the river about twelve feet behind the others.

They all rushed to them, and it was then that they saw what had caused the scream. Not more than fifteen feet out into the river, apparently caught on a rock was Meredith's purple clad body. She was face down in the water, bobbing gently up and down in the swells.

"Should we pull her out?" asked Kay. The _expression on her face indicated that she certainly hoped not.

"No," said Hattie, "We have to call the police." She attempted to use her cell phone without success. "One of us will have to go back to the inn and dial 9-1-1 at once. This is a dead zone. Oh, I didn't mean it that way," she stated hastily, gazing at Meredith's body, "I'll stay here with anyone else who wants to."

Elaine took off for the inn at a fast jog. The others stayed with Hattie, keeping an eye on Meredith's body. The rain continued to fall. All at once Meredith's body was dislodged by the current and washed farther out into the river to a deep channel where it disappeared beneath the surface.

"Oh no!" Hattie cried.

chapter fourteen

A Tinicum patrol car was the first to arrive with the Point Pleasant Water Rescue Unit right behind it. To Hattie's relief, Jim arrived just minutes afterward. He approached Hattie, "Tinicum and Plumstead will be working together" he said to everyone, "Please show me where you saw the body, who found it and anything else you found that would be pertinent."

The women gathered around him and started to tell him what had happened, "One at a time, please," he said politely, "Miss Hattie, perhaps you can begin." First Hattie told him in a rush that Meredith's body had been carried out into the river. She told him approximately where they had first seen the body. Immediately the five members of the rescue unit put their boat into the river and began their search. "The current in the channel is four or five times faster than the river itself," said one of the men to Jim. Hattie looked at her watch and saw that it was 5:15 when the search began.

For a moment Jim watched the boat as it went into the swift water. Forty-five minutes later two diving teams were dispatched and crews began to drag the river.

"Please fill me in on any details," Jim said to Hattie. She told him about finding her yellow umbrella and showed him where it was. Jim cocked his head and looked at Hattie strangely but said nothing. Then Elaine showed him the red hat bobbing at the water's edge farther along, and in the space between the umbrella and the hat Elsie and Kay pointed out where they had seen Meredith's body in the river.

"Thank you very much," Jim said, "And now I imagine you all would like to get back to the inn out of this rain. I'll join you up there later. We'll notify you as soon as we find the body." All wet and shaken, the women made their way back up to the inn.

When they entered, Eileen again ushered them into the front parlor and offered them towels to dry themselves with and more tea or coffee, "or something stronger if you wish." Some of them definitely wanted "something stronger." When everyone was settled Eileen turned to Hattie, "Miss Hattie," she whispered, "I'm so sorry about your friend. Leigh wants to see you in the kitchen." With that she accompanied Hattie back down the hall to the large and efficient kitchen.

"Oh, Miss Hattie, I am so glad to see you," said Leigh Wall, "I have some more information for you, I believe." Hattie nodded her head, and Leigh continued, "About 40 minutes after your friend went out, I was putting trash in the dumpster outside the kitchen door and I saw one of the Red Hat ladies going up the walk toward the parking area behind the house. She seemed to be soaking wet even though she carried an umbrella."

"What did she look like, Leigh?" asked Hattie.

"She had on a purple pants suit, high heels and a red hat with the brim pulled down low in front. I really could not describe her face."

"That's very helpful, Leigh, thank you. The police will want to talk to you when they come up here," said Hattie. She frowned to herself certain that the woman was the person whom Meredith had been following. What did Meredith know, if anything, about the woman? Why had she followed her? Was that woman the murderer? Why would she want to kill Meredith? Who was she?

While the women waited in the inn Jim, the other officer and two members of the rescue squad searched for some evidence of a scuffle along the trail. Not long after they commenced their search a homicide detective from the County arrived. Finally at a spot some feet north the umbrella, they found the grass and weeds flattened and the mud on the river bank churned up. "This is the spot where the struggle took place," said the detective.

chapter fifteen

Back at the inn, the first person whom Jim questioned was Leigh Wall, "Think hard, Leigh," he said, "Was there anything about the mysterious woman which struck you in particular?"

"Only that she was disheveled and very wet. Her umbrella was bent and kind of wrinkled, but it seemed good enough to help keep off the rain. And as I said, she was wearing red pumps with very high heels."

"You said that she was heading for the parking lot?"

"Yes, she was, but I couldn't see back there, and the rain was coming down very hard, so I came inside again and didn't pay any more attention to her."

"So, you didn't see her drive away, or what kind of car she was driving?"

"No, I didn't see her drive off, and I have no idea what kind of car she had."

He discovered subsequently that the mystery woman was the last to get there and the first to leave, so no one saw what kind of car she was driving.

"Did you see anyone else walking along the river or anywhere near the inn during the day?" asked Jim. "Not a soul," said Leigh, "I'm sure one of us would have noticed a stranger."

"Thank you," Jim said to Leigh, "You might have been a bigger help than you think."

Next he spoke with Eileen, "Did you get a chance to look at the thin woman while you were serving brunch?" he asked.

"This might sound stupid," Eileen said, "But after a while all of the women began to look alike, and I was working hard serving everybody! I mean, they all wore purple outfits and red hats, it was hard to pick anyone out in particular. I really didn't get a good look at the thin woman at all. I think that she was younger than the others, I can say that, but she had her hat pulled down on her forehead so far that I couldn't see her eyes. Oh, yes," Eileen said, "Did anyone tell you that Meredith Temple seemed to be following the woman?"

Jim asked all of the other women if they had noticed Meredith following the mystery woman. They were uncertain but thought she was. Their descriptions of the stranger were pretty much the same as Eileen's. When he got to Hattie, the only positive thing she could add was that Edie, Joyce, Elaine and Elsie were all taking pictures, but the slender woman was obviously reluctant to have her picture taken and turned away when she saw someone coming toward her with a camera.

Jim approached the four photographers and asked them for their cameras, "I promise that I will return them and your pictures as soon as I can." he said. They all turned their cameras over to him if a bit reluctantly.

In an effort to identify the mystery woman he asked Queen Mum Edie to give him the names of the other chapters who had been at the brunch and the phone numbers of their Queen Mums. "There were some members of only two other chapters there," Edie told him. She dug into her bright red purse and came up with an address book, "Here are the names and numbers of the two Queen Mums who were here,"

"Thanks a lot," he said, "These should be a big help." He copied the names and numbers into his notebook. Then he hesitated, "As I observe, women always carry their handbags with them," he stated.

"Oh my yes," said Edie, "We wouldn't be dressed without them!"

"Well then," he said, "where is Meredith Temple's purse?"

"She had a red leather bag with a shoulder strap," said Hattie, "I remember seeing it when we were leaving church and again at the Sunrise."

"Maybe it's somewhere in the river," Joyce suggested.

"Yes, maybe," Jim answered slowly.

"Jim," Hattie said, "would it be OK if we went home? To tell you the truth, I'm a little concerned about Wolf, and also Walter and Evelyn. They should be home by now."

"Oh sure," he said and turned to the others, "You may all leave now if you wish. I'll contact you as soon as we find Miss Temple's body. I must be going back, anyhow."

"Thank you," Joyce said, "Hattie, you come with me. I'll drive you home."

Three hours later and less than a quarter mile downstream, Sonar equipment detected Meredith's body caught beneath the walking bridge in Lumberville.

The Coroner and law enforcement officials rushed to the scene. The coroner asked the rescue squad to bring the body up from the river so that he could start a preliminary examination before it was zipped into a body bag for transportation to the morgue. Jim, the Tinicum officer and the County detective watched the Coroner closely as he worked over the soaking wet body of Meredith Temple.

After some minutes he stated, "This woman has a severe head wound, but I don't believe that was the cause of her death. She did drown, but after she was knifed several times in the chest. I'll be able to tell more when we get her to the morgue."

chapter sixteen

As soon as Joyce arrived at Hattie's they both saw her car parked in its usual place. There were lights on in the kitchen, and the outside light had been turned on, too.

"Everything looks so normal here, Hattie," Joyce said, "You could just about forget that anything horrible had happened today."

"You are right," Hattie said, but she suppressed a tiny shudder, "Would you care to come in?"

"No thank you, I'd best get home to my husband and sons," Joyce said, "But I'll take a rain check!"

"You have one," Hattie said, "And thank you so much for the ride home." She stood for a moment watching Joyce drive off toward the Pike Road. Where did that boy come from when he rode his bike up my lane from the Pike Road? She wondered.

Evelyn's voice interrupted her musings, "Auntie Hattie! Aren't you going to come in out of the rain? How was your brunch? Our lunch was wonderful. Hurry inside we have so much to tell you!"

I have so much to tell you, too, Hattie thought as she turned and walked up the porch steps and into her kitchen.

"You go first," Hattie told Evelyn and Walter.

"Oh Auntie Hattie," Walter said softly, "the entire Consistory was at lunch – six elders and six deacons. They asked me some very intelligent questions which I won't bore you with now. They were lovely people, really, four women and eight men."

"And," interrupted Evelyn, "they were very kind to me, too. We really had a lovely lunch. They made us feel so comfortable."

"When we finished our lunch, Pastor Schmidt told us kindly that they were about to have a meeting, and Evelyn and I left and came home."

"We knew, of course, that they were going to discuss us," said Evelyn.

"Of course," Hattie agreed, "When they have voted on whether or not they feel that you, Walter, would be right for the position of assistant pastor, and if they all vote "yes", they will take it to the congregational meeting in two weeks. Then the congregation will vote."

"Oh goodness," said Evelyn, "this is scary."

"Don't let it worry you, Dear," Walter said soothingly "This is just the way these things are done. I want to make it clear to you two right now, though, that if I am not unanimously approved, I'll not take the position. It would be too awkward otherwise."

"I understand," Hattie said.

"Now, how about your brunch?" asked Walter, "We've spent all of this time talking about ourselves, now it's your turn."

"Something perfectly horrible happened," Hattie said, "Meredith Temple was murdered!"

They both gasped. "How did that happen?" asked Evelyn, her eyes wide, "Please tell us all about it."

Hattie described everything that had transpired from the time she first saw the slender woman coming up the path to the Sunrise. "I know that it is not right to accuse anyone of anything, but I simply cannot imagine how anyone else there could have murdered Meredith. Nor can I figure out why anyone would want to." At that moment she was interrupted by the ringing of the phone.

She walked across to the counter and answered it. "Mrs. Farwell?" said a high feminine voice.

"Miss Farwell," Hattie answered emphasizing the 'Miss.'

"Miss Farwell," the high voice corrected, "I am Maria Stone from the Doylestown Globe. I understand that you were at the Sunrise Bed and Breakfast this afternoon with a group of Red Hatters when one of your members was murdered – allegedly by another. What can you tell me about this?"

"Miss Stone," Hattie said, "Please tell me who gave you that story?"

"Suffice it to say that I have it, and from a good source. I would like to talk to you about it. Our photographer is in Lumberville right now."

"Lumberville?" Hattie repeated.

"Yes," said Maria Stone, "They have just found Meredith Temple's body under the Lumberville walking bridge."

Hattie gasped, but she said, "Miss Stone, if you want any information about anything that happened today you will have to call the Tinicum Township or Plumstead Township Police or the County Detectives. That's all I can say. I'm sorry, but I have no information for you." Hattie hung up and turned to Walter and Evelyn, "I fear that this was just the beginning. The reporter told me that Meredith's body has been found."

Jim phoned then with the news about the body, where and

how it had been found and what the medical examiner had told them, "We'll know more tomorrow," he added.

"Jim," Hattie said, "I'm afraid that we will all be hounded by news people," and, of course, she was right. Television crews from Philadelphia and Bucks County hurried to the river even before Meredith's body had been located. Major newspapers had reporters and photographers there as well as did radio stations all covering the headline story which was dubbed, "THE RED HAT MURDER."

chapter seventeen

"Oh, Auntie Hattie," Walter said sympathetically the following morning at breakfast, "I am so sorry about your friend. What a dreadful way to go!"

"Yes it was," Hattie answered, "and something which sort of haunts me is how happy she was about going to the church service and the Red Hat brunch. She said to me last week, 'I'm looking forward to the entire day.' Who could ever have imagined how that day would turn out?"

"We never know, do we?" said Walter.

"Did she have any family?" asked Evelyn, "I realize that she was single, but what about brothers and sisters or nieces or nephews?"

"She was an only child," said Hattie, "I don't remember any aunts or uncles or cousins when we were little. Maybe some cousins do exist somewhere, but as far as I know there were none around here."

The phone rang, and when Hattie answered it she recognized the soft deep voice of her attorney. "Why Matt," she said in some surprise, "to what do I owe this honor?"

"I wish that I could say that this is just a social call," Matt answered, "but I'm afraid it's more serious than that. "Meredith Temple was a client of mine. I have a copy of her will here in my safe, and she has not appointed an executor nor has she left anything to anybody with the exception of her house, furniture and china which she bequeathed to the Church Home. Any money she had will also go to the Home after expenses have been taken care of. So that's pretty cut and dried. However, I am calling you because I know that you were long-time acquaintances, and I don't know if she had any other friends."

"Oh dear, Matt," Hattie responded, "I don't know of any close friends. She just joined the Red Hat society, but to my knowledge none of those women were old friends. Is there something that I can do?"

"Well, Hattie, I was wondering if you would mind planning her funeral. The funeral director, whoever you choose, will take care of the publicity. Of course, I will handle all of the legalities. I hate to burden you with this, but I thought you would be the most capable person I know to take care of it. Of course, there is enough money in the estate to cover the costs."

"I suppose that I can do that," Hattie said, "but did she say anything about where she wanted her funeral to take place, or where she wanted to be buried, or if she wished to be cremated or buried? Those things are important, aren't they?"

"It is important to abide by the wishes of the deceased," the lawyer said, "but it's really more important to the people left behind than to the deceased herself, isn't it? Unfortunately, Miss Temple didn't state her wishes to me, she just never got around to it, unless she wrote something and left it in her safe deposit box at the bank. We haven't opened that yet. I'll continue to search for any relatives, and I would appreciate your help if you don't mind."

"I'll do whatever I can," Hattie said.

"Thank you very much," said Matt, "I knew that I could count on you."

"When all of this is over with, Matt, I want to see you about re-writing my own will. A sudden death is an eye opener, isn't it?"

"It certainly is, and I'll be happy to help you with your will any time," Matt said pleasantly, "In the meantime, I'll stay in touch with you."

After they had hung up, Hattie turned to Walter and Evelyn, "As you probably surmised, that was my attorney. He has asked me to handle Meredith's funeral if we are unable to locate any relatives."

"We'll be glad to help in any way we can if you need us," Walter offered.

chapter eighteen

Jim and Benita showed up on Hattie's kitchen porch in the early afternoon. Hattie, as usual, was delighted to see them and immediately offered them something to eat or to drink.

They started to decline, but when they entered the kitchen they saw Evelyn and Walter sitting at the round oak table with large slices of chocolate cake in front of them. "The temptation is too great," said Jim and he and Benita joined the other two. He breathed in relishing the heady aroma of a recently baked cake.

"I just baked this cake," Hattie said as she served each of them and took a slice for herself. "Coffee, tea or iced tea?" she asked.

Once they were all settled, Jim told them the results of the autopsy, "The coroner said that the wound he found on Meredith's head was caused by a blunt instrument of some sort. It might have been a heavy stick, he said. However, she had been stabbed six times in the chest – deep knife wounds which penetrated her heart and left lung. He said that she was still alive when her assailant pushed her into the river. So the cause of her death was actually drowning, although she would have died anyway.

"Now," he reconstructed the scene, "her assailant approached her from the rear and knocked her out with that blow to her head. Then she stabbed her with a sharp knife before she dragged her down to the water. We are assuming that her killer was a woman."

"Who else could it have been than the thin woman in the red hat?" asked Hattie.

"She is the logical suspect," Jim said, "and the women at the inn said that they didn't see anyone else out by the river or anywhere else all day."

"Does anyone have any idea about her identity?" asked Benita.

"I've talked to all three of the red hat queen mums. Of course Edie Rapp said right from the start that she had no idea who the woman was, but neither of the others did, either. In fact each of them thought that the woman was a guest of one of the other chapters. I also talked to the women at her table, and they all said that they had never seen her before. In addition I asked Leigh and Eileen if they had seen a handbag anywhere which fit the description of Meredith Temple's. They both stated that they had not seen any handbags that anyone had left behind. "

"I wonder why Meredith was so interested in that thin woman," said Hattie, "Of course, being Meredith, she was curious about everyone, but she kept staring over at that woman. She said that there was something familiar about her or something like that, but she couldn't place where she had seen her before."

"You told us that she jumped up from the table when she saw that the woman had gone," said Evelyn, "Apparently she wanted to get a closer look at her or even confront her. I wonder why."

"She never said," Hattie stated, "I wonder, though, if the thin woman was really after Meredith. This is so strange. Maybe she left the room figuring that Meredith would follow her. Maybe she believed that Meredith knew something about her that she didn't want anyone else to know. Maybe she'd planned to kill her all along."

chapter nineteen

Benita glanced quickly at Jim and he returned her look.

"Well," said Jim, "The lab does not have too much information on the muddy footprints on your kitchen porch, Miss Hattie, and even less on the baseball bat. Maybe we'd better clear up one mystery at a time!"

"Oh dear," sighed Hattie. She turned to Evelyn and Walter and told them about the mysterious young boy and all of the nasty happenings with which they thought he was involved, including the injury to Officer Dolan of which they knew.

"The shoe prints on your porch were made by boys sneakers, and they were size 8," Jim told her, "There was nothing on the baseball bat which could be used because the finger prints were too smudged. The same is true of any DNA.

"A boy's shoe size 8 would be a girl's size 9," said Benita, "so his feet are not real big."

"I have a hunch, Miss Hattie," said Jim, "that you are possibly still in danger. Please be aware, and don't go wandering around alone."

"Why do you think someone is still after me?" asked Hattie, "I suppose Wolf is still in danger, too."

"I don't want to take any chances," said Jim.

"There is one thing which disturbs me, too," said Benita, "That is your yellow umbrella. No one could question the fact that the umbrella is yours. What if the killer thought Meredith was you?"

"Oh no," protested Hattie, "why I wasn't even wearing a red hat."

"That's true," said Jim, "But you said the room grew dark during the storm, and you were sitting two tables from the slender woman, and even Eileen said that everyone began to look like everyone else."

"What if she wasn't concerned about the purple outfit and red hat?" said Benita, "What if she saw someone with a yellow umbrella following her and thought it was you? According to the M.E. she smashed the heavy stick into Meredith's head from behind."

"Do you carry that yellow umbrella often, Auntie?" asked Evelyn.

"Every time I go out in the rain," said Hattie, "That would be to the grocery store, shopping and to church. I lent it to Meredith Sunday afternoon after we left the restaurant. And yes I did carry it out of the restaurant before we saw Meredith. Do you actually believe that someone has been spying on me?"

"I have no idea," said Jim, "But it is possible."

"Why? For Heaven's sakes why?" asked Hattie, "I simply do not understand this at all."

"Whatever the reason," said Walter, "Until we know for sure that no one is after you, and that you are safe, we will keep an eye on you at all times."

A little smile played around Hattie's lips, "Thank you all so much," she said in a soft voice.

"I feel the urge to do some investigating," said Benita. She dabbed at her mouth with a paper napkin, "The cake was wonderful, Miss Hattie, Thanks a bunch." She and Jim left, and Evelyn rinsed the dishes and put them into the dish washer. Hattie had never felt more loved and protected.

chapter twenty

The next morning Evelyn was in the kitchen making coffee when Hattie descended her pie crust steps. "My goodness, Evelyn," Hattie said in surprise, "What got you up so early? It's not even five o'clock!"

Evelyn smiled broadly, "We went to bed early last night. I had quite enough sleep, and don't forget that it's almost 10 o'clock in England. Anyway, I was hoping to have the coffee made to surprise you." She turned the coffee maker on, "There! But now it's no surprise."

"Thank you, Dear," Hattie chuckled, "and it really was a very pleasant surprise to find you here. Now I will take Wolf out for a little walk." She stepped over to a hook next to the door and lifted wolf's leash from it.

"Auntie, may I go with you?" asked Evelyn.

"Of course," said Hattie, "As long as I can be assured that you are not just guarding me."

Evelyn laughed, "I'm afraid that I would not be much good as a guard."

The sky was brightening when they left the porch, but the

sun had not yet risen. A light mist rose from the ground and hung in the trees.

"It's beautiful here," said Evelyn, "I simply love it."

"Let's walk in the woods," Hattie suggested. She and wolf led the way across her lane and onto a path she often used in the woods. They were greeted by the damp smell of the earth and the scent of wild flowers. The birds were just welcoming the day with their morning songs.

"This is heavenly," Evelyn sighed, "One misses so much when living in the city."

They walked a little way until Wolf had performed his duty and Hattie said reluctantly that they had best return to the house. They were almost to Hattie's lane when wolf growled, a deep and threatening rumble. His ruff stood up and he stopped walking.

He turned his head toward the lane as if he were looking through the trees and bushes. He growled once more.

Then they both saw what he was growling at. The boy in black was speeding down the lane on his bicycle. He slowed at Hattie's parking area and spun into it next to Hattie's car, the only car there. In his hand he held a baseball bat.

Wolf suddenly charged toward the boy, breaking Hattie's hold on his leash. Both women ran after him, but by the time they reached him he had the boy flat on his back and was standing over him growling ferociously. The boy screamed. The women yelled at the dog, "No, Wolf, no," cried Hattie, but Wolf refused to budge.

Aroused by the hubbub Walter came racing out onto the porch. He took the three steps in one bound and raced to the dog and terrified boy. He grabbed Wolf's collar and with difficulty pulled him away while the women started to help the boy to his feet.

They were greeted by a string of profanity such as neither

had ever heard. All the while he was swearing the boy was roughly pushing them away and rushing to his bike. He grabbed his hat from the ground, and before they could stop him he was on his bike and out of sight around a bend in the lane. He left his bat lying where it had fallen.

Hattie and Evelyn simply stared up the empty lane while Walter took Wolf into the kitchen. "That boy is not right in his head," Hattie observed, "I am more convinced now than ever that he is the one who bound Wolf's legs and mouth with masking tape and beat him nearly to death. It is obvious to me that Wolf knows that, too."

They hurried into the kitchen where Hattie went over the dog carefully. "He seems just fine," she said in relief.

"I checked his mouth for blood to make certain that he did not bite that ruffian, but thankfully there is no sign of that," said Walter, "May we take your car up the lane and see if we can find where the boy went?" asked Walter.

"That is a wonderful idea, Walter," said Hattie, "Let's go!" She hurried into the kitchen for her keys while the others jumped into her car.

There was no sign of the boy on the lane. "He's a speedy bike rider, I must say," said Evelyn, "Maybe he's hiding in the woods."

"That's possible," Walter agreed, "but he is speedy and he had a bit of a head start on us."

Hattie had her suspicions about the boy's destination, but just in case he was living in one of the Victorian-type houses in the development, she drove around the roads there. There was no sign of life outside any of the houses, and other than some lights in second floor windows, there was no other indication that people were anywhere around.

They saw no bikes at all.

"I think that we'd best tell Jim about this episode," said

Hattie, "At least as far as I'm concerned the boy does not live in the development."

chapter twenty-one

Jim and Benita arrived at Hattie's house about a half an hour after she phoned them with her story. "Since you seem convinced that the boy does not live in the development," Jim said to Hattie, "there is not much question in my mind or yours, I am sure, that the boy is Alice Farnsworth's grandson, and that he lives with her. I believe that it's time for me and one of the other officers to pay a call on Mrs. Farnsworth."

"Yes," added Benita, "And don't you think that the slender mystery woman is Mrs. Farnsworth' daughter, Jayne?"

"This is indeed a tangled web," said Walter.

"It would certainly seem that the thin woman was Jayne," said Jim with a frown, "But I just don't know."

"What do you mean, you don't know?" asked Benita in confusion, "Who in the world else could it be?

"That's a very good question," said Jim.

Hattie stared at Jim for a long moment. Finally she said, "You have an idea which you are not sharing with us, don't you Jim? Tell us, please, who do you think the slender woman really is?"

I'll tell you once I have interviewed Mrs. Farnsworth and had a chance to talk to her grandson. Maybe things will clear up then," he said.

"Pardon me for sounding mysterious, too," Benita said, "But I have some things I want to investigate, and I have asked Terri to come over and help me with them. You see, there is nothing I can do officially since I took a leave of absence from the FBI, but Terri is still active with the Special Investigations Unit in Philadelphia, and she should be a big help."

"We'll see, we'll see" said Jim.

chapter twenty-two

On the following morning at about 10:30 a young man who identified himself as a process server appeared at Hattie's front door bearing a subpoena for the removal of her "dangerous, part-wolf, dog." It stated that "This vicious animal attacked an innocent young boy named, Ronny Wellington, who was simply making a call on the dog's owner, Miss Hattie Farwell. "The wolf-dog", it continued, "ripped the young boy's clothing, in particular his sleeve, and bit his arm so savagely that he had to be treated in the Emergency Room of Doylestown Hospital. Furthermore," the subpoena stated, "Miss Farwell allowed the dog to run free where it presented a hazardous condition to any persons walking or riding their bikes nearby."

Hattie was rendered speechless. She turned to question the process server, but he had disappeared before she could really see him or find out who had given him the subpoena. She handed the subpoena to Walter who had just walked up behind her. "My word! Auntie!" he gasped, "this is all lies. I think that you had better call your lawyer at once."

"Just what I was about to do," Hattie said. She returned to the kitchen and dialed Matt's number. When she reached him he said, "I'll be right over. Don't do anything until I get there."

She did only one thing, she called Jim. "I'm coming right over," he said.

Jim arrived first and was outraged when he read the subpoena. "None of this is true!" he stated. "the subpoena does not say when the 'young boy' was treated at the Doylestown Hospital ER, but I'll check on that."

Matt knocked on Hattie's kitchen door right then, and she hurried to let him in and show him the subpoena. Wolf limped over to him and licked his hand.

"Is this the vicious wolf/dog?" asked Matt with a laugh.

"Oh Matt," said Hattie, "what am I to do? I'm so afraid that the animal control officer will come over and take Wolf away."

"We won't allow that," Matt stated forcefully.

"Someone, and we believe it was that young boy, Ronny, fastened Wolf's paws together with masking tape, and taped his mouth shut. Then that person beat the dog almost to death with a club of some sort." She reached into a box on her counter and pulled out a card which she handed to Matt, "This is my veterinarian. He took care of wolf after the police found him on the Pike Road. You can talk to him."

"Why Would anyone do a thing like that?" asked Matt in shock."

"We suspect that the Farnsworths have a vendetta against Hattie for some reason," said Jim. There have been other attacks or attempted attacks. As a matter of fact one of our police officers, Don Dolan, was struck with a baseball bat thrown at him deliberately by that boy, or one who looked like him."

"One who looked like him?" Matt repeated, "What does

that mean? Have you seen other boys around who look like him?"

"No, no," said Jim, "that was a dumb thing to say. We haven't seen any other boy around here at all."

"Can you identify him when you see him?" asked Matt.

"We've never seen his face," said Hattie, "He wears a baseball cap with the brim pulled around backward and low on his head. Also, he has so much hair hanging around his face that he would be impossible to identify. Meredith said that when she saw him in the super market with his grandmother he was also wearing dark aviator sunglasses."

"Meredith?" asked Matt, "Do you mean Meredith Temple?"

"Yes," said Hattie, "Meredith Temple, my Red Hat friend who was murdered. She told me several days ago that she had seen Alice Farnsworth and her grandson in the 611 Super Market."

"The poor woman was the victim in the so called Red Hat Murder case," said Matt, It has really received a lot of publicity. What a tragedy. We discussed it on the phone, of course, Miss Hattie. As I told you, Meredith Temple was a client of mine.

"Well, I'm afraid we have strayed from the subject," Matt continued.

"Maybe a little," said Walter, "but there is something you should know. There was apparently a mysterious woman wearing a Red Hat outfit at the brunch at the Sunrise. She was walking on a path by the river, and Miss Temple was seen following her by many of the women. It was on that path that Miss Temple was murdered and thrown into the river. Some suspect that the murderer was Jayne Farnsworth."

"Perhaps that's something to go on," said Matt, "What does she look like?"

"We don't know," said Hattie somewhat sheepishly, "She

kept her had pulled down so low over her face that no one could see her features."

"The pictures the Red Hat women took are at headquarters now. Maybe we can make out something from them," said Jim, "Most of them were taken with digital cameras and the pictures are clear."

Matt sighed deeply, "OK," he said, "Is it your opinion that either the shy mother or her shy son sent the subpoena?"

"Yes, unless it was Alice Wellington Farnsworth, Jayne's mother. But somehow I do not believe that she sent it," Hattie said.

"Why not?" said Jim, "She certainly made it obvious that she was furious with you about something, that day in church."

"Tell me," Matt ordered, "what Sunday was that?"

"It was a week ago this past Sunday," said Hattie, "That very rainy day when the river was flooding. Anyway, she came rushing down the aisle with the altar flowers in her arms and bumped right into me. When I tried to talk to her she told me not to speak to her 'after what I had done.' I have no idea to this day what I had done. I haven't seen or heard from her since."

Well," said Matt, "I think that a visit to Mrs. Farnsworth and her daughter and grandson is definitely called for. I'll also ask them which one filed the suit against Miss Hattie. I'll phone her and try to make an appointment to see her this afternoon. In addition, I think that you, Jim, should find out what you can about a young boy treated at Doylestown Hospital Emergency Room for a dog bite. All the details, please, when, how severe, was his clothing torn? You know."

"Yes, I know," said Jim. He rose to leave, "I'll get on it right away."

"And I'll call Mrs. Farnsworth now," said Matt, "May I

use your phone, Miss Hattie?" He lifted the receiver without waiting for an answer.

chapter twenty-three

To Jim's subsequent astonishment there was no record of any young boy being treated for a dog bite in the Doylestown Hospital emergency room in the past month.

"Maybe somehow the record has been lost in your computer," he suggested. The clerk's response was rapid and decisive, "No way!"

He checked with the doctor on duty on Wednesday, but he stated that he had treated no boys for dog bites that week or even in the past month. Afterward he checked with the other local hospitals with the same result.

He shared the information with Benita when he went home. She was equally confused, but told him of a plan, "I'm going to call Terri at once," she said, "If she can't get out here, I'll go to Philadelphia. I'm anxious to investigate the Farnsworths. That is a very strange family."

Matt was unable to reach Alice Farnsworth on the phone, but a woman answered who identified herself as Jayne. "My mother isn't available right now, Mr. Borzio," she said, "Is there anything that I can do to help you?"

"Perhaps you can, Miss Farnsworth," he answered, "I would like to call on you at your home today if possible. I am also anxious to meet with your son, Ronny. Will you both be available at about three o'clock?"

"I'm not certain," she said hesitantly, "I'll be happy to meet with you, but I believe that Ronny has gone out in the car with my mother. If they get home in time, they will both be here."

"We'll just have to go along with that arrangement for the time being," he said, trying not to sound disappointed, "I will be meeting with the others some other time."

Feeling a trifle cowardly Matt phoned Jim and asked him to go with him to the Farnsworth home. "I'll be glad to go," Jim said, "Frankly I think that is a wise move on your part."

When they arrived the double wrought iron entrance gates were wide open, and they drove through. There was no sign of Alice Farnsworth's car in the driveway. "It looks as if they haven't returned yet," said Jim, "I am looking forward to meeting Jayne, though."

It was obvious that the mansion was not occupied, but there were three workmen's trucks parked in the circular drive in front of the house, and when Jim and Matt left the car the sound of hammering from inside the house could be heard clearly.

"What a beautiful home!" said Matt. The center portion of the brick house was three stories high. A wing extended out on either side, and each was two stories high.

"It's elegant, isn't it?" said Jim. He looked at the pillars in front of the center section and the white painted woodwork on the entire house. I believe that it is at least 200 years old.

"Meredith Temple said that Mrs. Farnsworth told her they would be staying in the gardener's cottage until the house was ready, so I guess we'd better look for that." he said. The men had started walking along the driveway past the right wing of the house when a woman approached them.

She was very thin and wore navy blue shorts and a long-sleeved flowered blouse. Jim judged her to be about five feet six inches tall in her flat-healed sandals. Her hair was brown and naturally curly. "Hello," she said pleasantly, "I'm Jayne Farnsworth."

The men introduced themselves, and Jayne invited them to the gardener's cottage where they could talk. She led them down the driveway past an elaborate six car garage which appeared to have living quarters above it. "Does anyone live up there?" Jim asked nodding to the second floor of the garage.

"No," said Jayne Farnsworth, "The chauffer and his family once lived there, but that was a long time ago, and it's a terrible mess now. My mother no longer has a chauffer." She picked up her pace, and the men lengthened their strides as they followed her.

A narrow flagstone path led away from the driveway and through an arbor draped with wisteria. Jayne pushed at the vine impatiently, "This must be cut back," she stated.

Once through the arbor, no more than 25 feet away they saw a charming little house, painted white with dark green shutters. Across the front was a porch with a hammock at one end and rocking chairs scattered along it. Black-eyed Susans stretched in front of the porch and beyond it into the yard.

"How charming," said Matt, "It looks like a picture in a children's book. Has anyone been living here recently?"

"Yes," said Jayne, "The former gardener was given life rights to the place when my grandparents died. He painted it and kept it up until his death about five months ago. I understand from my mother that he was close to 90. His name was Peter Barry."

"The name doesn't ring a bell with me," Jim said.

"No, I wouldn't think so," Jayne said, "Mother said he was

reclusive. He had no family, but he just loved this little cottage and its gardens. Apparently he left the estate only when it was absolutely necessary."

"How fortunate for you and your family that he kept it in such good condition," said Matt Borzio.

"I know," Jayne nodded her head, "Please, come in and I'll fix some tea. Or would you prefer coffee?"

"Tea is fine with me," said Jim as he followed her inside. "Me, too," Matt said.

They entered a small, cozy living room with a fireplace at one end and a staircase against the wall leading straight up to the second floor at the other end. Jayne led them through the living room to an even smaller dining room and into the kitchen at the back of the house. She put the kettle on the stove and gestured for them to sit at a tiny wooden table near the back door.

Matt came directly to the point, "Miss Farnsworth, did you sue Miss Hattie Farwell because of her big dog?"

Jayne looked shocked, "No!" she said, "I didn't even know that she had a dog. I never saw it."

"Apparently someone named Farnsworth did," he said, "Or someone made up a subpoena to scare her with. A process server delivered it to her this morning."

"I cannot imagine that it was my son," she said, "He's just a young kid."

"Did he have a torn shirt and severe dog bite marks on his arm?" asked Jim, "Did you have to take him to the emergency room at Doylestown Hospital?"

Jayne looked shocked, "No," she said. She handed them their tea and placed lemon, cream and sugar on the table.

Jim and Matt looked at one another in confusion.

"Another question," Jim said, "Did you know Miss Meredith Temple?"

"Who?" she said, "I don't remember meeting her."

"She was a member of the Country Gardeners chapter of the Red Hats. She was murdered Sunday on the river bank near the Sunrise Bed and Breakfast where they all had been having brunch." Jim said.

"I read about that in the paper," she said, "That was horrible. Poor lady."

"Did you go to that brunch dressed in a purple pants suit and a red hat?" asked Matt.

"No! of course not," she exclaimed, "Why would you even think such a thing? I didn't attend the brunch at all!"

Matt took a long sip of his tea, "Sorry," he said.

"I think it's time for us to go," Jim stated, "Thank you for your hospitality and the tea, Miss Farnsworth. I hope you'll grant us permission to come again."

"Of course," she said graciously.

Matt glanced at the stairs to the second floor as they walked through the living room, "How many bedrooms do you have?" he asked.

"Two and one little bathroom," she answered, "My mother and I share one bedroom and my son has the other. It's pretty tight quarters, especially for my mother. We'll all be glad when the big house is ready."

"I'm sure," said Matt, "Goodbye, Miss Farnsworth, and thank you."

She walked them back to their car much to their disappointment. Jim barely glanced at the garage as they walked past it, but he would have loved to have had a chance to see inside it. Maybe soon, he thought.

chapter twenty-four

While Jim and Matt were at the Farnsworth estate, Hattie, accompanied by Evelyn, went to the funeral home to make arrangements for Meredith's funeral. The coroner had called that morning to say that the body was ready to be released, and when Hattie conveyed that information to the funeral director he told her that he would pick up the body and handle everything subject to Hattie's advice.

He said if Hattie wanted a viewing he would need an appropriate outfit to put on Meredith. Hattie thought that over carefully and decided that Meredith would probably like that, so she and Evelyn drove to Meredith's home to find a suitable dress.

The front door was barred by police tape, and an officer stood by demanding to know their business there. Hattie handed him a note from the funeral director. The officer unlocked the door and they entered the house. The officer followed them in.

Despite the heat of the day, Hattie shivered when they were inside, "It feels so empty and cold in here, almost as though Meredith had never been here at all," she said. Evelyn hugged herself and nodded in affirmation. When they reached Meredith's bedroom they were greeted by the stale smell of her powder and perfume. The same was true of her closet when they were selecting her dress for the viewing. "Oh dear," Hattie sighed, "It's all so final isn't it? I'm very anxious to leave." "Me too," Evelyn agreed. The guard followed them back outside.

Hattie and the funeral director selected the following Sunday afternoon for the viewing at the funeral home. Then Meredith's body would be cremated, and Monday morning at 11 o'clock was scheduled for the funeral at Trinity Church, conducted by The Rev. Arnold Schmidt. Fiona agreed to play the organ. Hattie and Evelyn planned a small reception in the Parish House following the service. The funeral director placed the obituary in the papers, and Hattie was almost finished with her chores. Meredith's death affected her more that she had imagined.

When they arrived back at Hattie's house Jim took one look at Hattie and said, "You're looking a little pale. How about if I call Benita and ask if she can stop at the Italian Restaurant on the way over here and pick up some spaghetti and meat balls? And perhaps a bottle of chianti?"

"Oh Jim." said Hattie, "You are so thoughtful. I love your idea, chianti and all!"

"Will you stay, Matt?" asked Jim, "We will have a lot to talk about."

"I'd really like to, thanks," said Matt, "Would you believe that this is my day off?"

When Benita arrived she had not only two bottles of chianti, and a large order of spaghetti and meatballs and rolls, but she surprised everyone by bringing Terri along. Hattie embraced Terri, "I feel as though I have come home again," said Terri with a happy smile. She greeted Evelyn and Walter, hugged

Jim, and Hattie introduced her to Matt. Wolf bounced around her as best he could.

chapter twenty-five

Following their dinner everyone remained seated at the kitchen table, because as Jim had said earlier to Matt, "We have a lot to talk about."

Hattie started the conversation by telling Matt all about the plans for Meredith's funeral. "Thank you more than I can say, Miss Hattie," Matt said, "You have planned a very suitable send-off for your friend.

"I contacted the Church Home two days ago", he continued, "and they are planning to send a truck to Miss Temple's house on Saturday to pick up her furniture. They didn't know how to divide Miss Temple's jewelry, she had some lovely pieces, so they have planned to auction them off along with the furniture they can't use and her car. They will also auction the house and the rest of its contents. The notice will be in the papers tomorrow through Sunday, and a sign will be posted outside her house."

"This is a sad time," said Hattie, "I'll call your office and make an appointment with you to re-write my will this week!"

"Don't talk that way, Auntie!" said Evelyn, "I don't want to hear it."

"Ignoring things won't make them go away, Dear," Hattie told her, "Anyway it will make me comfortable, even if I live to be 100!"

"Tell us all about your visit to the Wellington estate," Benita said, "Did you see Alice Wellington Farnsworth? Or did you meet her bratty grandson? How about Jayne?"

Everyone leaned forward, listening, "We met Jayne," Jim said, "nobody else."

"How come?" asked Terri, "I'm disappointed."

"So were we," said Matt, "but according to Jayne her mother and son were out somewhere in her car. She didn't tell us any more than that."

"She invited us into the gardener's cottage where they are living until the mansion has been properly repaired. Maybe that will be soon, because we heard hammering inside and three trucks were parked in the drive," Jim said, "You were right, Miss Hattie, that is a magnificent place."

"What condition was the gardener's cottage in?" asked Hattie.

"Great!" Matt exclaimed.

"Jayne Farnsworth told us that the former gardener had been left life rights to the cottage in the Wellington's wills, and he really kept it up beautifully. He cleaned it, painted it, fixed it up where needed and worked in the gardens. He was about 90-years-old, though, when he died, so he had slowed down some," Jim said.

He turned to Hattie, "Maybe you knew him, his name was Peter Barry."

"Peter!" said Hattie, "I saw him only occasionally when he went to the store, but he never socialized. He had the reputation of being a recluse. But," she continued, "he wasn't always like that. When we were young, teenagers and even in our twenties, he was one of the handsomest men I had ever seen. He was eight or nine years older than we were, and we loved to hang around him. On top of that he was a marvelous gardener. He knew everything there was to know about plants and flowers."

"Really?" said Benita, "What did he look like?"

Hattie smiled, remembering, "He was tall and slim. Maybe not quite six feet, but he held himself beautifully. He had a nice sense of humor, too."

"And?' questioned Benita.

Hattie laughed, "He had brown curly hair and hazel eyes. There isn't much else to say. As far as I know he never married. He just stayed on at the Wellington's. After awhile he became only a hazy memory until you just brought him up."

"Let's get back to Jayne Farnsworth," Jim said, "We asked her if she knew Meredith Temple, and she said she had never heard of her. When we reminded her that Meredith had just been murdered, she said, "Oh, yes, I read about that in the paper. Poor thing," or something like that. She was very casual."

"She denied having anything to do with the Red Hats, "said Matt, "and she also said that she knew nothing about the subpoena. Indeed, according to her, her son was never bitten by a dog. Also she claimed that she didn't know that you even had a dog, Miss Hattie."

"How strange," said Hattie, "How very strange. Did you notice anything suspicious about her?"

"No, nothing," said Matt, "She was friendly, conversed easily and was a welcoming hostess. She was quite attractive, too, in a skinny way."

"She showed us her first floor, gave us tea at her little kitchen table and seemed very nice," said Jim.

"How interesting," Terri said.

chapter twenty-six

"Who delivered the subpoena?" Matt asked.

"He told me he was a process server," said Hattie, "I didn't get a good look at him, because he stood in the shadows when he handed me the subpoena. As soon as I started to read it I was so shocked I forgot the young man entirely. I did turn to question him at one point, but he was gone."

"Could you identify him if you had to?" asked Matt.

"No," said Hattie, "I'm sorry but I didn't pay attention to him."

"Could you identify him, Walter?" asked Jim.

"No, I'm sorry," He answered, "I'm afraid that I never saw him. He had just handed the subpoena to Auntie Hattie, and I was very concerned with her reaction to it. She started to read it then turned around toward the porch, and there was no one there."

"Was he driving a car or truck?" asked Matt.

Neither Walter nor Hattie had seen how he got there or how he left. They both stated that there was no vehicle in her lane. "Maybe he parked down the lane or on the Pike Road," Hattie said.

"I'll check on the subpoena if I may have it," Jim said. He held out his hand for the subpoena. "Maybe if we're real lucky, we'll find fingerprints on this thing."

"I don't know what's wrong with me," Hattie said, "I'm usually much more observant than this."

"That subpoena was very shocking," Jim said kindly, "Especially after what you had just been through with Wolf."

"Don't make excuses for me, Jim," Hattie said. She placed her elbows on the table, put her head in her hands and closed her eyes.

"Please, don't take it so hard, Auntie," Evelyn said.

"No, no, that's not what I'm doing," Hattie said lifting her head "I'm trying to remember." She shut her eyes again and replaced her head in her hands.

Everyone looked at her, but no one said anything more. Suddenly Hattie opened her eyes, raised her head and lowered her arms to the table. "I do remember something!" she stated, "The young man was wearing a brown jacket similar to the uniform jackets worn by the United Parcel Service employees. His pants were brown, too. His brown hair was slicked straight back from his face. He wore eyeglasses with wire rims. His eyebrows were bushy and full and he had a small mustache. How's that?" she said with pride, "and, oh yes, he was about five feet six inches tall."

"Wow!" said Jim, "You don't have to worry about your memory!" He hesitated for a moment, "Now I have a hard question for you. Is it conceivable that the process server was actually Ronny Farnsworth wearing a disguise? Think about it. Take your time."

For several long moments Hattie said nothing. Finally she took a long deep breath before she answered, "I believe that it is possible. Furthermore he came to my front door. Maybe a process server would do that, but also Ronny knew that Wolf would be in the kitchen."

"Oh, my gosh!" said Benita, "Could he have made up the subpoena? A young kid like that?"

"Yes," said Matt, "I think that he could have. You would be amazed at what some young kids can do. He undoubtedly used a computer."

"I wonder if we have enough evidence to get a search warrant for their house," said Jim.

"I'm afraid not," said Matt, "But maybe something else will turn up. Just keep them in your sights."

Terry had taken out a notebook and was busily writing in it. She said nothing.

There was another silence. Jim shifted in his seat, sighed and said, "I have had something else on my mind for some time."

Benita stared at him, "I knew it!" she exclaimed, "Let's have it. We won't think you're foolish, I promise."

Jim laughed, "You can't speak for the others. Maybe they'll think I'm crazy!" He looked at everyone else.

"Will you please spit it out?" Matt said, "We won't think you're crazy, will we?"

"No!" chorused Hattie, Benita, Terri, Walter and Evelyn in unison.

"See?" said Matt, and they all laughed.

"O.K. here it is," said Jim, "I think it's possible that the skinny woman in the purple pants suit and red hat – the woman who might possibly have killed Meredith Temple, was actually Ronny wearing his mother's clothes."

His theory was greeted by a collective gasp.

"Think about it. Meredith said that she didn't get a good look at him in the grocery store, but she certainly got a better look than anyone else did. She told Miss Hattie that there was something familiar about the woman. Something she could not put her finger on. Could she suddenly have realized that the skinny woman was really Ronny?"

For a moment they were all silent as they tried to digest Jim's idea.

Finally Benita spoke up, "What about those high heels? Could a thirteen-year-old boy actually walk around in three-inch heels?"

"I don't know," Jim said, "But if I'm correct he did! Maybe he had been practicing."

"No matter what, he is a very dangerous boy," said Matt.

chapter twenty-seven

For the next two days there was no sign of the boy, Ronny, or anyone else in his family. The auction at Meredith's home had been scheduled to begin at 7:30 AM on Saturday, and Benita, Terri, Evelyn and Hattie decided to attend. Walter, who showed no interest whatsoever, said he would stay home with Wolf, and Jim was on duty. Matt called on Friday and told them he felt obligated to go and would meet them there.

The day dawned clear, cool and sunny, but the weather forecast was for temperatures in the mid-80s by afternoon. Benita and Terri (who slept on the couch in Jim's and Benita's apartment) arrived at 7 o'clock promptly and found the other two awaiting them on Hattie's kitchen porch.

"I'll drive," offered Terri after all of the 'good mornings'. Hattie and Evelyn climbed into the back seat and they drove off immediately. When they reached Meredith's road they were astonished to find many cars parked along both sides of the road as well as in the side streets.

Why don't you take a chance and park in the parking lot

at Elsie's apartment? asked Hattie, "I'll go up and knock at her door and see if she wants to go with us,"

"I hope she does," said Benita, "otherwise, I don't think it would be right for us to stay in her lot." A guard made that very clear when he tried to stop them from entering, and also chased other cars away.

Elsie, as it turned out was happy to see Hattie at her door, "I was going to phone you," she told her, "I take it you are going to the auction, and I would love to go too. Obviously we'll have to walk, but it isn't too far."

While they were walking a television truck drove past them, "That seems ghoulish to me," Hattie sighed. The TV people joined other news people in front of Meredith's home. They stood around talking and joking with one another. Hattie sighed again, "Of course they never knew Meredith."

They made their way around the house to the open garage where the auctioneer had set up a long table. He and his helpers busied themselves with the items they planned to auction off first.

"Will you be auctioning off Miss Temple's car?" asked Evelyn. "Oh yes, everything goes." Said the auctioneer. Evelyn turned her head as the large box truck from the Church Home drove past and down the driveway.

"The Church Home people took everything they wanted now," the auctioneer said.

"But," said Hattie softly, "they will enjoy the proceeds of the auction after everything has been sold."

"Don't you approve of that, Auntie?" asked Evelyn.

"Oh, yes I do," said Hattie, "I honestly cannot think of a more deserving charity. It just makes me feel kind of funny to see all of the things Meredith cherished over the years displayed as they are for others to pick over."

"I understand," Elsie said, "But they are just things."

"And if some of those things make someone else happy, I think that's a good thing," Benita said.

"You are wise beyond your years, Benita," Hattie laughed, "Oh, here's Matt. Good morning," she said to him.

"I'm here to observe," he told them, "I want to make certain that everything goes as it should."

chapter twenty-eight

Back in Hattie's kitchen, Walter had just poured himself another cup of coffee and was about to carry it out onto the porch when Wolf growled ferociously. The dog's ruff was up, and he stared through the screen door in the direction of the parking area.

Walter pushed the great dog back from the door and quietly slipped out onto the porch where he stood hidden behind a large cedar tree. What he saw through the branches made his blood boil. The young boy in black was aiming a baseball bat at Hattie's parked car.

After a moment's hesitation Walter decided to go back into the kitchen and dial 9-1-1 before he attempted to stop the boy. There was no doubt in his mind that the boy was quite mad, and he wanted to make sure that police back-up was on the way before he approached Ronny.

The person who answered his call assured him that help would be right on the way, and with that knowledge he opened the door and ran down the steps. "Stop that, Ronny!" he called out. He started toward the parking area as Ronny turned suddenly and charged toward him with the bat raised.

The first thought which crossed Walter's mind was that the boy had not yet smashed the bat into Hattie's car! His second thought was that if the police didn't arrive very soon that bat would be smashed into him! He looked around desperately for a weapon when suddenly Wolf burst through the screen on the kitchen door and charged toward Ronny.

Walter didn't know whether he was more frightened for the boy than he had been for himself. Once again Wolf knocked Ronny to the ground and stood over him snarling down into his face. And once again, the boy screamed – a strained and high pitched screech which was almost feminine in its urgency.

Walter raced to the dog and grabbed his collar, but Wolf was too strong to drag away from Ronny immediately. Wolf continued to snarl and Ronny continued to scream.

Then a police car pulled up with its lights flashing and the siren competing with Ronny's screams. A new young officer jumped from the car, and with his gun drawn pointed it directly at Wolf!

"NO! NO!" yelled Walter, "Don't shoot the dog! He was just protecting the car from the boy. He would never bite anyone, really! That boy was just about to smash his baseball bat into Miss Farwell's car. This is Miss Farwell's dog, Wolf."

The officer kept his gun raised. "Shoot him, shoot him!" yelled the boy through gasps of terror, "He's a vicious wolf/dog!! Kill him! Kill him! Can't you see how mean he is?"

The young officer hesitated, but his gun remained pointed at the dog. Wolf exposed his fangs, and his growling grew fiercer. There was a distinct 'click' as the officer pulled back the safety catch. "NO!" shouted Walter, "don't shoot Wolf!"

And then there was the loud 'BANG' of a gun being discharged.

Startled, the young officer spun around toward the sound,

his gun still drawn. Jim was behind him, his smoking gun in his hand. "Replace your safety!" Jim ordered, and the young man did. Jim strode toward Walter, "I don't usually perform so dramatically," he said, "but I was afraid we were about to lose Wolf, so I fired a shot into the air." He replaced his gun in his belt.

"Thank God you came," said Walter, "And I do mean that reverently."

"What shall we do with this young terrorist?" asked Jim.

"I doubt if you have any grounds on which to hold him," Walter said regretfully.

"Nope, not yet," said Jim, "Maybe if we give him enough rope he will hang himself!" Walter pulled Wolf away from Ronny, and Jim told the boy to go home. As he had before, Ronny slapped his cap down farther on his head, grabbed his bike and rapidly rode off up the lane. That time he did not swear.

chapter twenty-nine

The auction was going well. Kitchen items were put up first, and Benita bid on some new dish towels, a set of plastic glasses and some china plates. She also bid on an electric grill and can opener. No one in the crowd seemed interested in those items, so Benita was able to purchase them for very little money, a fact which delighted her.

Terri's primary interest was in the jewelry, and when that was auctioned off she pushed close to the auctioneer. But she faced stiff competition from some eager women whom she heard state that the jewelry was their reason for coming. They outbid Terri on almost every item, but she was successful when she bid on a jade ring and matching bracelet. On impulse she also bid on a brown leather purse. To her delight, only one woman bid on the purse but gave up early.

"This must be the way gamblers feel," Terri stated, "Once you get something, you want to keep on bidding on more."

"That's true, and Terri, I must tell you that the jade jewelry just matches your eyes!" Benita said. She turned to see what was up next, "Ooo!" she said, "How do you like the handmade patchwork quilt that's just coming up, now? I love it! What luscious colors, all shades of blue, rose and green." She waved her hand in the air, "Ten dollars," she bid. Another woman bid fifteen, and another twenty. "Twenty five dollars," called Benita. "Thirty," shouted one of the others, "Thirty five," yelled Benita. And so it went until Benita finally won it at one hundred and twenty dollars. "It's really worth much, much more than that," she said happily as she gathered it into her arms.

Hattie, who had declared all day that she was not interested in bidding on anything, changed her mind in the late afternoon when Meredith's crystal animal collection was put on the block. "Oh, look," Hattie breathed, "There's a dog that looks very much like Wolf. I would like to own that!" She raised her hand when the bidding started.

She found herself up against some stiff competition in the bidding, but she made up her mind not to give up. When she reached ninety-five dollars, Matt leaned over and asked her, "Miss Hattie, is this for the dog alone or the entire crystal collection?"

"Just for the dog, Matt," she answered, "But he's worth it!" No one else bid any more money on the dog, so Hattie paid for it and it was hers! "I like auctions," she announced as she admired her new purchase.

"Shall we leave now?" asked Evelyn, "Or does somebody want to bid some more?"

"I do," stated Benita, "I want that car."

"My goodness, Benita, what will Jim say if you get it?" Hattie asked.

"He'll be thrilled, I know," Benita answered. Just then the bidding started, and she threw herself into it with complete abandon. On the bidding went, up, up and up. Then suddenly it stopped at three thousand nine hundred dollars, and the Toyota was Benita's.

"It's a bargain!" she squealed, "A real bargain! I'm going to call Jim. She pulled out her cell phone and pushed Jim's number. To Hattie's surprise he apparently was as delighted about the car as was his bride. "He's coming right over!" said Benita.

Benita just remembered that Evelyn had purchased nothing the entire day, "Oh, Evelyn," she stated, "I forgot that you didn't bid on anything. I hope that you weren't bored to death."

"No, not at all," said Evelyn, "I enjoyed it all. It was great fun."

The bidding on the house had commenced, and they all watched with interest while they waited for Jim. "If I thought we were going to stay here, I might be interested in bidding on the house," said Evelyn, "It is very attractive."

The bidding became quite furious. "Don't worry Evelyn," Hattie consoled her, "Something much better will come along."

Finally the house and almost two acres of land sold for just over $300 thousand. "A steal," mumbled Evelyn.

When Jim arrived he hugged Benita and rushed right away to see the car, "It's a beauty," he declared, "You did get a real bargain. A three-year-old Toyota in good shape is worth much more than you paid." He hesitated a moment, "It is in good shape, isn't it?"

"The auctioneer told me that everything he sold was "as is." But it looks great, doesn't it? and I'm sure that Miss Temple took real good care of it." Said Benita.

"I'll take it to the service garage right away to be gone over," Jim said, "I'm sure it will be fine. May I have the keys please?"

He checked out the interior of the car, including the glove box. Then he examined the engine, "It all looks just fine to me," he said as he walked around to open the trunk.

The others followed him to the car's rear and stared in horror when he opened the trunk. "Good Lord!" said Jim, "there's a woman's body in here!" He checked her pulse, but she was obviously dead.

Hattie leaned forward and looked at the body, "That is Alice Wellington Farnsworth!" she cried, "Who killed Alice? Why? And who put her body in this trunk?"

"And how was that accomplished without anyone knowing?" asked Terri.

Jim went over to question the auctioneer. But he had no idea of what had happened or how. "We inspected the car last evening, locked it up, closed the garage doors and locked them, too," said the auctioneer.

"Don't leave," Jim ordered the auctioneer and his helpers before he called the coroner.

chapter thirty

After the body had been taken to the morgue, and the car to police headquarters for evidence of fingerprints and DNA, Jim questioned the auctioneer once again as well as his shocked helpers. Jim was convinced that none of them had any idea that there was a body in the car's trunk or how it got in there. "We eyeballed the entire Toyota last night when we were organizing the auction," the auctioneer repeated in a dazed tone, "That included opening and looking into the trunk. There was absolutely no sign of anything amiss. This is the first time anything like this has happened at any of my auctions, and it's just horrible."

"Was the set of keys you gave my wife the only set for the car?" Jim asked.

"Yes," said the auctioneer, "the house keys were on a separate ring."

"Keep yourselves available," Jim told the men and dismissed them once he had their names and addresses.

He watched as detectives searched the garage where the car had been parked before he climbed into his police car and drove over to Hattie's house.

Once in Hattie's kitchen they all seated themselves at their usual places at her round oak table. Everyone was anxious to talk, but Walter started the conversation, "I had a phone call today while you were all at the auction," he began, "It was from Mr. Jones, the president of Consistory. Their vote for me, and Evelyn, was unanimous! The Parish meeting will be in two more weeks, and then we'll know for sure if we are to stay here."

"Congratulations!" said Jim. "Yes, congratulations!" echoed Benita. "I'm certain that the congregation will want you, I really am," said Hattie. "I do hope so," said Walter. "And so do I," said Evelyn. "That's something I'm going to add to my prayer list," Hattie said. "Amen," Walter added.

"Walter had an adventure today, too," Jim said, "That boy, Ronny, came back again with a baseball bat."

"But fortunately Wolf stopped him from bashing your car, Auntie. Jim and I will tell you all about it later," Walter said, "And oh yes, Jim repaired your screen door."

"You'd better tell me all about it later!" stated Hattie.

"Now," said Benita, "would everyone like to see what I bought at the auction?"

"Sure," Jim said, "I'm anxious to see how you spend my hard earned money!"

They all laughed, and Benita punched him in the arm. She opened the plastic bag with the dish towels, and then she showed them her can opener and electric grill, the plastic glasses and the china plates. "They cost me next to nothing," she bragged.

"Unlike the Toyota with the corpse in the trunk!" he whispered in her ear.

She pretended to ignore him and showed off the handmade patchwork quilt. "Isn't it beautiful?" she asked. Everyone, including Jim, admitted that it was.

"Terri, you go next," said Hattie, "You made a good buy, too."

Terri smiled and happily showed off her new jade jewelry, "I really love it," she said, "And it will just match a dress I bought last week. "Also," she continued, "I bought this beautiful leather handbag." She showed it to everyone, "Now, Miss Hattie, show us what you bought."

Hattie pulled the crystal dog from a plastic bag, and holding it tenderly she displayed it to everyone around the table. "I think that it looks just like Wolf, and it is beautiful, isn't it?" Everyone agreed that it did look like Wolf and that it was beautiful. "Don't patronize me," she scolded, "Now I want to find a special place for this dog."

After spending several minutes looking around the room she said, "The mantle piece will be just perfect." She strode over to the fireplace and carefully placed her new crystal sculpture next to the antique clock on the wide wooden mantle.

chapter thirty-one

Terri pulled her notebook from her purse, "I have a few things to tell you all," she said, "With the help of some of my colleagues at headquarters, I have done some research on Alice Wellington Farnsworth. You might be surprised at what I've learned. In addition, I have had a chance to look through this leather purse. It did not belong to Meredith Temple. It belonged to Alice Farnsworth!"

"My word!" gasped Hattie, "How do you suppose it wound up at the auction?"

"A very good question," said Terri, "but before we delve into that mystery, I want to disclose what was in the purse. She held up a yellowed newspaper clipping. This contains the picture of Alice and Anthony Farnsworth at their wedding." The picture showed a pretty, slim bride smiling at her new husband. He, too, was smiling. However, he was far from handsome, short and very overweight. "I didn't get to their wedding," Hattie said, "and I had never seen Anthony Farnsworth. As I recall they met in school in Virginia, but I'm a bit surprised that he, well, I don't want to seem unkind, but I'm surprised that he looked as he did. Of course, he might have been extremely personable."

"Yes," said Terri, "It might interest you to know that he was also extremely wealthy." She looked through a fat notebook which she had taken from the purse, "This is a diary, which believe it or not, Alice kept for years. However, she did not write in it every day. From this book in addition to my research, I learned that Alice and Anthony were both 32-years-old when they married. They moved to Colorado where he had established an extremely successful leather business." Terri cleared her throat, "You'll also be interested to learn that not quite seven months after their wedding Alice delivered an eight pound baby girl whom they named, Jayne. The diary gives a brief account of a trip home several years later when Alice brought Jayne to see her parents. That was the only time she came back home as both of her parents died shortly after her visit. However, there was a notation in the diary which read, 'Peter drove to the airport to meet us this morning, and he was very happy to see us both. I admit that I was thrilled to see him again, too, especially when my parents were nowhere around! I have always missed him and always will.'"

"Good grief!" said Hattie, "I should have guessed that Peter was the father of Jayne. Alice was always crazy about him. Her parents would never have permitted her to marry Peter, so obviously when they found out that she was pregnant, they arranged her marriage to Anthony. Or so it appears."

"Yes," Terri said, "There is more. I believe that Benita and I have uncovered the reason she was so angry at you."

"You have?" said Hattie, "Please tell me."

"We judge from the diary," Benita said, "that at one time in your youth, you promised Alice (or so she believed), that you would never sell your upper pasture to a developer. According to the diary, when she came back and went up to her old bedroom, she saw nothing of the lovely view she had once enjoyed from her window. Instead all she saw, in her words, was 'rows and rows of houses filling the wonderful open pasture I always loved.'"

"Oh dear!" said Hattie, "I simply cannot recall ever having such a conversation with Alice. Anyway, my parents and my brother would still have been alive "in my youth." Maybe when we were very young something like that was said, but I really don't remember. Poor Alice."

"Another thing," Benita said, "Didn't Meredith tell you that Alice had said that her husband died 'a couple of years ago'?"

"Yes," Hattie said.

"Well, he didn't," said Terri, "He was killed in a hunting accident almost fourteen years ago!"

"You're kidding! said Jim.

"That book doesn't look big enough to have carried diary notes for years," Hattie observed.

"No", said Benita, "Most of the pages are missing since the death of Anthony Farnsworth."

"That would be nearly fourteen years of missing pages," said Hattie.

"Yes." said Terri, "and I guess that we are all thinking the same thing. As I figure, Jayne would have been in the early stages of her pregnancy with Ronny, perhaps two or three months along, when Anthony was killed."

"Is there anything in the diary about Jayne's baby? Is there any mention of who the father was?" asked Matt.

"Not exactly," said Benita, "but Alice did write that Jayne had been seeing a man neither she nor Anthony liked for about a year, and then one day she told them she was pregnant."

"Alice wrote that Anthony was livid," Terri said, "She wrote, 'Anthony just said the nastiest thing to me that he has ever said. He sneered, 'like mother like daughter!' According to her diary, Anthony didn't want a hint of scandal to touch his family. His business was a huge success, and he had made some powerful friends.

" Jayne told us point blank that she is not about to be married," Alice wrote, "and she says, 'I am not going away, either!' Anthony is in a rage. He constantly orders Jayne to abort the baby, and she very sweetly tells him 'no', but Anthony won't give up." Sometime later Alice wrote, "If Anthony hadn't been shot to death I don't know what would have happened! But it has been six months since he died, and Jayne has given birth to Ronny. He is an adorable little thing, and Jayne and I both love him to pieces."

"Have you any idea of what happened to Ronny's father?" asked Evelyn.

"There is no further mention of him – not his name nor his whereabouts. Nothing," Terri said.

chapter thirty-two

The following morning Jim and Benita went into Hattie's house with her when they drove her home after church. "I won't keep you," Jim said, "I know you will be busy preparing for Meredith's viewing this afternoon, but I have some news for you." Hattie leaned forward expectantly, "I assume it's about Alice Farnsworth," she said.

"Yes," Jim stated, "the autopsy has been completed. Incidentally, Alice had some foreign matter caught in her hair which proved to be straw, as would be found in a straw rug. She was wearing an expensive pair of brown leather shoes which matched the bag that Benita bought at auction. She also looked as though her mouth had been taped shut, and there were similar marks on her wrists."

"But most important of all was the fact that she had been stabbed in the chest numerous times. That is what killed her," Benita finished for him.

"Her car was found in her garage," said Jim. Walter and Evelyn pulled Hattie's car into her parking spot right then. "Oh Auntie Hattie," Evelyn said happily when they entered the kitchen, "Did you notice? Everyone was so nice to us at church."

"Yes," said Walter with a wide smile, "But we can't let ourselves become too optimistic."

"Well," Hattie said, "The parish meeting will be next week, so we don't have much longer to wait."

"We were just talking about Alice Farnsworth's autopsy," Jim said, "She was stabbed to death. We haven't found the murder weapon, yet, but I'll be going to the Wellington estate this afternoon with some detectives to see what we can find. And believe me, we'll find everything we are looking for if we have to dig up the entire estate!"

"Where's Terri? asked Evelyn.

"She had to go back to Philadelphia early this morning. She said to say 'goodbye' to everyone, and she'll be back as soon as she can." Said Benita.

chapter thirty-three

Evelyn and Hattie went to the funeral home at two o'clock, two hours before the viewing was set to take place. They thought that Meredith looked lovely and that the dress they had selected was perfect. There were ferns spread out behind the coffin and sprays of flowers sent by friends, including Hattie. Hattie was satisfied.

"Would you like me to put out coffee and tea?" asked the funeral director, "I usually do if the family wants it. I'll put out some cookies, too, if you'd like."

"That would be just lovely," Hattie told him,

"Meredith would approve of that." Suddenly she felt very tired. She sat in a chair in the first row and stared at Meredith in her coffin. Evelyn sat down next to her, "Are you all right, Auntie?" she asked in a concerned voice.

"Thank you, dear, I'm fine. But I keep wondering, why anyone would want to kill Meredith? What could she have possibly done to make someone want to kill her?" She wracked her brain going over and over everything Meredith had told her about seeing Alice Farnsworth and her grandson in the market.

She went over the Red Hat brunch at the Sunrise and the thin woman in a Red Hat outfit. And she wondered again about the strange fascination Meredith had with the thin woman and the way she followed her along the river path. Followed her to her own death. Then she reconsidered Jim's theory that the thin woman was really Ronny dressed in his mother's outfit and a red hat. Could that 13-year-old boy really be a killer? She believed that he had meant to kill Wolf. Had he killed Meredith? Why? Had he killed his own grandmother?" She sighed heavily.

"Hattie," said a woman's soft voice. Hattie returned to reality and stood to hug an old friend. Then the room filled up, and there was no more time for wondering. When it was over Evelyn said, "It went very well, Auntie."

"Yes, thank goodness," Hattie answered, "If the funeral goes as well we can breathe a sigh of relief." We can go early tomorrow and take tea sandwiches, coleslaw, potato salad, rolls, cold cuts and deviled eggs to the refrigerator in the parish house. A number of the women are going to bring food, too, especially pies. We can set up the coffee urn and put the kettle on for tea and put table clothes and napkins on the tables." Evelyn patted her arm, "Don't worry Auntie Hattie, everything will be just fine. I'll help you all the way." Hattie smiled at her and gave her a loving hug.,

"You'll make a wonderful pastor's wife, darling," she said.

chapter thirty-four

"Now," said Jim to the other detectives, "the police have a legal right to search the Wellington house and estate." He displayed his recently acquired search warrant. As soon as they went through the double gates they saw Jayne Farnsworth walking toward them. It was just 7:30 on that warm Monday morning.

"Hello, Lieutenant," she said politely, "I guess that you are here because of my mother's death. It was very kind of you to come up and break the news to me yesterday. Thank you."

"You are welcome, Jayne. I have a few questions for you now if you feel you are up to it. Have you any idea who would want to kill your mother? Or why?"

"No, I told you that yesterday. I cannot think of any reason anyone would want to harm her in any way. I'm just beside myself."

"I'm sorry," Jim said, "this must have been a terrible shock for you and your son, too. By the way, where is Ronny now?"

"I don't know," Jayne looked perplexed, "He's been here all

day. I don't know where he went. He was completely broken up over his grandmother's murder."

"Of course," Jim commiserated, "Well, while we are waiting for him to come home we'll just look around." He produced the search warrant and handed it to her. The first place he chose to search was the gardener's cottage. He looked back up the driveway, and saw that Jayne was still standing in the same place, staring at the search warrant in her hand. Chief James Sabath, of the Tinicum Township Police, joined him as he entered the cottage, and together they searched through the first floor and then climbed the stairs to the second. It was as Jayne had described, two bedrooms, one for Ronny, and one which she and her mother shared. There was also one small bathroom just as Jayne had said. Ronny's room was the first one that they entered. It was decidedly a boy's room. The closet contained black jeans, a black sweatshirt, a black jacket, black sneakers and a black baseball cap. There were boy's pajamas and underwear and socks in a bureau. A single bed was made up with a striped bedspread over striped sheets and a pillow case.

"Nothing exciting so far," mumbled Chief Sabath. The second bedroom was larger. There were two closets, each filled with women's clothing. A large chest of drawers contained women's underwear in separate drawers. Nowhere did they find such Red Hat clothing as a purple pants suit, a red hat or a pair of red shoes with very high heels. Jim went through the closets once more, and although he found several pairs of sandals and flat heeled shoes, there were no shoes with high heels in either closet. Other than the chest of drawers the only other furniture in the room was a pair of twin beds. They were made up with pink sheets and bedspreads. The bathroom cabinet contained only soap, toothpaste, deodorant, combs and brushes, pain killer and emery boards. In addition to the usual towels and wash clothes, three toothbrushes hung on a rack on the wash stand. There was nothing else. "Three towels, three wash clothes," said Jim." There were clean sheets and towels in a linen closet in the hall. Nothing else.. A trapdoor in the ceiling led to a crawl space. Jim swung himself up into it, "Nothing up here," he said. All of the floors in the house were random width pine upon which braided throw rugs had been placed. There was no basement, just another small crawl space under the house, and that was also empty.

"It's funny," said Jim, "This place is amazingly uncluttered when you consider that three people lived here."

"Yes," agreed Sabath, "I was thinking that. This must be a very neat kid. I have a twenty-year-old daughter at home, and her room is a mess even when she cleans it!"

chapter thirty-five

"Now," said Jim, "let's go look at the garage." The only car in the garage had been the Porshe belonging to Alice, and it had been taken to the forensics garage the previous day. The detectives looked around at the floor for suspicious stains, but found none. Upstairs, though, there was a different story. It smelled dusty, dust puffs stirred on the floor when the door was opened, and most telling of all was the fact that the floor was covered with straw rugs.

"Look at that!" Jim exclaimed as he pulled on his latex gloves, "I believe that Alice Farnsworth was kept a prisoner up here, for at least one or two days." He scraped dust and straw from the rugs and placed them into an evidence bag.

"This would explain the straw and dust in her hair for sure," stated Chief Sabath, "Yes," Jim agreed. They continued to search the good-sized apartment with the other detectives. In a small closet tucked away in a back room Jim found a brown jacket and matching pants. In the jacket pocket was a pair of wire rimmed glasses. "Well here's proof that Ronny was the process server!" he exclaimed. He put the clothes into an evidence bag.

"Look here, Lieutenant!" one of the men called out, "Aren't these the high heeled red shoes you were looking for?"

"I'm sure that they are," Jim said, "Have you found any other clothing? In particular I am looking for a red purse, a red straw hat and a purple pants suit." Jim placed the shoes in another evidence bag.

"While you look up here," said another detective, "I'm going to look through all of their trash and even their garbage (ugh!)" He hurried downstairs. In one small bedroom Jim found a single bed made up with white cotton sheets, "Where did you find those shoes?" Jim asked the man who had found them.

"It was strange, Lieutenant," said the man, "I almost didn't see them. They were hidden beneath a loose floorboard under the bed."

"Hmm," Jim mumbled, "I'd better have a closer look at those shoes." He pulled them from the evidence bag, and still wearing his latex gloves, he looked them over thoroughly. "The heels are all banged up," he said, "Now why would that be? According to the Red Hat women there was nothing wrong with the shoes. They would have noticed bangs and scrapes as severe as these." He searched the floor and woodwork in the room until he came to the window sill. The sill was banged and gouged along its entire length. "Look here, James," he called out, "It looks as though the shoes were used as hammers. Someone, obviously Alice Farnsworth, was trying to attract attention." Then he remembered the persistent hammering which he and Matt had heard when they visited Jayne, "We thought it was the workmen inside the mansion," he said, "and of course some of it was." He shook his head, " I'm so sorry that we didn't look up here then", he added, "we might have saved her life." He felt awful.

"Here, I'll bag the bed sheets from this bed," said the chief, "and the towels, too."

"Good," said Jim, "Thanks." They piled the sheets and towels into an evidence bag, "I'll just have another look around," Jim said. He walked slowly from room to room looking into every closet as he went. He also looked under the beds and felt for loose floorboards, but he found nothing more." When they were back outside Jim noticed the other men digging through the trash cans next to the gates. He was about to climb into his car when Jayne Farnsworth approached, "Will you be wanting to talk to me anymore?" she asked.

"No, Miss Farnsworth, I have no further questions for you right now," Jim told her.

"In that case, would you object if I went back to the cottage to lie down for a little while?" She pressed her right hand against her temple. Jim looked at her closely. She had dark circles under her hazel eyes and she seemed ill, "Please, do lie down, Miss Farnsworth," he said gently, "You need your rest. We'll be looking around here just a little while longer, but we won't need to talk to you again today." She looked relieved, and she smiled at him gratefully.

"Thank you," she said. Jim was very anxious to find the purse, purple pants suit and red hat that the slender woman had worn to the Red Hat brunch. So far there had been no sign of any of them. He and the men were also searching for Ronny's bike with no luck there, either. Jim walked over to the men who had dumped out the trash can. With their gloves on they searched through every piece without success. Finally they put the trash back into the container and dumped out the smelly garbage can.

"This is no fun!" grumbled one of the men. He picked up a gooey, messy hunk of something leather, and exclaimed, "Lieutenant! I believe that I have found the red purse!" Jim hurried over to look at the thing, "You're right!" he said, "See if there is any identification inside." The man shoved the soggy shoulder strap aside and unzipped the bag. Fortunately the inside was relatively dry and untouched, and in it was Meredith's wallet containing her license, her credit cards and her key case. "We'll just check these keys," Jim said,

"but I believe that the duplicate car and garage keys are here." A few minutes farther into the search through the garbage, one of the men drew out a smashed red straw hat and shortly thereafter the sodden purple pants suit, which was actually plumb, as they later realized.

"There is no sense in bothering Jayne Farnsworth right now," said Jim, "Let her sleep. It's her son, Ronny, whom we need to talk to!" He looked at his watch,

"Where does the time go?" he asked rhetorically, "It's almost one o'clock!"

chapter thirty-six

At that moment, outside the servants' gate, Ronny was digging behind thick bushes to retrieve his bike. As usual he was wearing black. Black pants, black shirt, black sneakers and black hat. His hat was on backward as always. He jumped on his bike and rode rapidly off toward Hattie's lane. No one was home yet at Hattie's. Meredith's funeral had started at 11 AM, and the church had been crowded. Although he did not wear his Roman collar, Walter did attend the service with Hattie, Evelyn and Benita. Matt joined them in their pew, "Did you see all of the Red Hat ladies coming in?" he whispered. The women turned and looked at the back of the church where most of the women in the Country Gardeners

chapter were finding seats in back pews. They all wore their purple outfits and red hats. Pastor Schmidt conducted a lovely service. Meredith's ashes were in a golden urn at the front of the church and the pastor's prayers were personal and heartfelt. Hattie secretly applauded him for that since he barely knew Meredith. After the service everyone went to the Memorial Garden for the interment of the ashes. Later when the congregation was gathering for lunch in the parish house, the pastor said to Edie Rapp,

"Wearing your Red Hat outfits was a lovely tribute. Miss Temple would have been very pleased." The meal was served buffet, and Hattie and Evelyn were relieved to see that there was enough for everyone. Walter ate somewhat rapidly and excused himself immediately afterward.

"Why is Walter rushing off?" asked Hattie.

"I honestly have no idea, Auntie. He must have something on his mind." Evelyn had a puzzled look on her face when she stared at the door through which her husband had vanished, but she just shrugged her shoulders. Jim, who missed the funeral service but arrived during the lunch, noticed the concerned look on Walter's face when he was eating his meal. He thought he'd be wise to follow him. When he arrived in the parking lot, he saw Walter stepping into Hattie's car and went over to him.

"I believe that I know what's bothering you, Walter," he said, "Here, get in my car we'll go together. When the ladies are ready to go home, they can use Miss Hattie's car." He ran back into the parish house to give Hattie her keys but rushed out again before she could ask any questions. He drove directly and rapidly to Hattie's house. When they arrived they saw Ronny's bike in Hattie's parking area but no sign of the boy. Jim parked his car and both men jumped out and ran up the steps to the kitchen porch. The door was wide open, and although he was out of sight, they could hear a string of swear words which could have been coming from no one but Ronny. Jim pulled his gun and told Walter to stand back while he went into the kitchen. Over the noise of Ronny's swearing Jim could clearly hear the low rumble of Wolf's growl. Ronny was slowly approaching the great dog with his baseball bat held high. "Halt!" ordered Jim, "Halt, Ronny! "Don't make me shoot you!" The boy turned toward Jim and slowly lowered his bat, but he kept the dog in sight constantly. Suddenly out of the corner of his eye he spotted the crystal dog on the mantle, and with a maniacle laugh he charged across the floor to grab it. Wolf lowered himself to a crouch, but he didn't move, he simply growled. "This'll make the old bitch sad!" yelled Ronny. He took his eyes from Wolf just long enough to reach for the crystal dog. Wolf sprang at him and knocked him to the hearth before his fingers touched the model. Ronny's baseball bat clattered to the floor. Jim grabbed Ronny by the arm and hauled him upright. Walter ran into the room and pulled Wolf away. "I suddenly was overwhelmed by a terrible fear for Wolf," said Walter, "I guess that sounds silly, but I just had to get back here."

"No, it doesn't sound silly," Jim assured him, "I kind of felt the same fear myself." Jim looked at the boy, but in spite of his standing so near, he still couldn't make out Ronny's features as well as he wished. The boy's hair was, as usual, all over his forehead, eyes and most of his face.

"Ronny, why are you so angry at Miss Farwell?" asked Walter in a soft voice.

"She made my grandmother cry!" he said, "She made her very sad because she put all those houses in the pasture. My grandmother cried and cried and cried. That's why! She wouldn't stop crying. I had to stop her! And now she's dead, and it's all Miss Farwell's fault!!" Unexpectedly Ronny pulled away from Jim and ran outside. The men followed him, but he had climbed on his bike and ridden off so rapidly that they failed to stop him.

"I know where he went," said Jim, "He's gone back to his mother, I'm sure. He has never threatened her, so I think she'll be OK for a while. I'll go get him soon enough."

"It would seem," said Walter, "that he killed his grandmother, apparently to keep her from crying. But why did he keep her a prisoner in the garage? And why did he kill Miss Temple?

Did he fear that she would recognize him? I guess he explained why he wants to hurt Auntie Hattie through Wolf."

"I don't know," said Jim," but before I do anything more I want to phone the lawyer whose name and number Jayne gave to me. Then I want to get hold of a good psychiatrist. Dr. Eunha Kim is a psychiatrist now at Doylestown Hospital. I met him several years ago before he passed his psychiatric boards. He was a general practicioner then and he's a very fine doctor.

"Anyhow, when we have Ronny in custody at police headquarters, I would like Dr. Kim to have a talk with him. I hope he can explain what's wrong with the boy."

"And," Walter added, "I pray that he can help him."

chapter thirty-seven

The Wellington lawyer, Theodore Prime, answered his phone on the first ring. Jim identified himself and asked him if he was still a practicing attorney. When Mr. Prime said that he was Jim told him the sad story of Alice Wellington Farnsworth and her daughter, Jayne, and her grandson, Ronny.

"I cannot remember ever meeting Jayne Farnsworth or her son, but at one time I knew Alice quite well. You see, my father was their attorney before he retired. He and Alice were about the same age. I did not know Anthony Farnsworth either, really, but I was at his and Alice's wedding. Alice kept in touch with me sporadically over the years, and I was very sorry to learn from her of her husband's tragic death. Fortunately I was also able to help her with the legalities."

"Is there anything which you can tell me that would help us in our investigation into Alice Farnsworth's death?" Jim asked.

"No, I'm sorry," said Mr. Prime, "that would be a violation of attorney client privilege."

"Of course," said Jim., but he wondered what Mr. Prime knew.

"Is there anything you can do now for Jayne?" he asked, "Except for her wild and vicious son, she is really all alone in the world. It's strange, isn't it? There she is with that beautiful home and estate and no one to share it with."

"Hmm," mumbled the attorney, "I'll have to call her about the reading of her mother's will. Maybe when I talk to her I can figure out a way to help her. You see, Alice Farnsworth's will is in my safe."

"Oh good," Jim said, "Mr. Prime," he continued, "If Jayne hires you as her attorney, and I imagine she will, she will probably need you very soon." Theodore Prime raised his eyebrows but said nothing. He just waited for Jim to continue, "Jayne's son admitted to me and Walter Whyte, a pastor, that he had killed his grandmother. He has done other awful things, and we believe that he also killed a friend of Walter's aunt, Hattie Farwell, a woman by the name of Meredith Temple. I won't go into further detail now, but it will be necessary for me to arrest the boy very soon. I thought that perhaps you would like to be present when we bring him in to police headquarters."

"That will depend, of course, on whether or not Miss Farnsworth wants me," said the lawyer.

chapter thirty-eight

As it developed, and to no one's surprise, Jayne did ask Theodore Prime to be her attorney. Late that afternoon he met with her privately in the den in the mansion and read her mother's will to her. He explained to her that she was her mother's sole heir, and that all of her mother's money and possessions would now belong to her.

"But, Mr. Prime!" she exclaimed, "That can't be right! What about Ronny? Mother loved him a lot, she would never have left him, her only grandson, out of her will! This has to be a mistake!"

"There is no mistake, Jayne," Theodore Prime said softly,

"Why? Why?" Jayne cried, "This is very wrong. What will Ronny say when he finds out? What will he do?"

"Do you intend to tell him, Jayne?" Theodore Prime asked. His tone was very gentle.

"I guess I'll have to," Jayne answered with tears streaming down her face, "He should be here very soon." Theodore Prime left the room and went in search of Jim. "Lieutenant," he said,

"There is something you should know. Would it be possible to get Dr. Kim to come over here at once?"

"What's up? Jim asked.

"Jayne Farnsworth is a very disturbed woman," Theodore Prime said, "Much more disturbed than you might suspect."

"I'll call him immediately," Jim said, "Are you afraid that she might hurt herself?"

"Yes, or worse," said Prime. Dr. Kim didn't hesitate when Jim called, "I'll be right over," he said. When he rang the doorbell, Prime let him in, "We're in the sitting room off the den, Doctor," he told the psychiatrist. Jayne is in the den, and she's very disturbed."

"Can you tell me what has upset her?" asked the doctor, "Has anything happened just recently?" Prime described her hysterical reaction to the reading of Alice's will. "She said that it was very unfair to Ronny. She said that she would have to tell him."

"Yes, I see," said Dr. Kim quietly. At that moment the double doors to the den burst open, and Ronny charged through them, "What the hell do you mean by not giving me my inheritance?" he roared, "All of you can go to hell! Get out of here, damn you, before I smash you to bits!" He hit one of his balled fists into the palm of his other hand. "My grandmother would never leave me out of her will! That's got to be just a rotten trick!" He turned and ran back into the den. Dr. Kim followed Ronny into the den and began talking to him very calmly.

chapter thirty-nine

There was no more that Jim could do then, and he returned to headquarters where he had work to catch up on. He gave Theodore Prime his cell phone number and asked him to please call him as soon as the doctor had finished with Ronny. Back in his office he collected copies of the pictures that the four Red Hatters had taken at the brunch. He was still waiting for the reports from the police Forensics Unit and the results from the fingerprints in the garage. He called Forensics and gave them Hattie's phone number. Benita and Terri met him in Hattie's kitchen where they were joined by Walter and Evelyn. Jim handed the pictures to Hattie first. She examined them closely and shook her head,

"That is definitely the thin woman in her purple pants suit and red hat, but you cannot see her face."

"No," said Jim, "I've called Eileen and Leigh and the women who took these shots. They should all be here within 20 minutes or so." Hattie put on a pot of coffee while they waited.

"Most of my pictures are pretty good, if I do say so myself," said Edie when she arrived, " but there is no way I can tell what she looks like."

"I'm sorry," said Joyce a half hour later when they had all gathered around the table, "that woman can't be identified from any of my pictures." Elsie and Elaine stared at all of the pictures, but the mystery woman could not be identified, "She turned her head away every time she saw a camera coming," said Elaine, "I just can't figure out anything about her that's identifiable." Eileen and Leigh also stared at each picture carefully. Eileen sighed deeply, "I was hoping that I would be able to help you, but it's hopeless." she said. Leigh nodded her head in agreement. Jim handed the pictures to Terri and Benita, "Is there any way that we can see her better?" he asked.

"I'm afraid there aren't miracles of that kind yet," said Terri.

"Well, my men have found the red hat and purple pants suit that she most likely wore as well as the high heeled shoes. We'll see what DNA shows up." said Jim.

"In the meantime I'll get some of my guys over here to dust for Ronny's fingerprints around the other side of the room where he stood earlier when he was threatening Wolf."

"Poor Wolf," Hattie said, "It's amazing that he isn't completely traumatized."

"It really is, Auntie Hattie," said Walter, "That young boy came at the dog on more that one occasion with a baseball bat. And Wolf is such a nice dog. Why does Ronny want to hurt him so?"

"I hope that Dr. Kim will be able to sort all of that out," said Jim, "That boy is the angriest person I have ever seen. He's consumed with hate it seems."

"I just can't imagine what kind of a life he has led that has turned him into such a monster," said Benita.

"It's not safe to let him run loose in society," said Evelyn. She turned to Jim, "Won't he have to be put away?"

"I don't think that there could be any other alternative," said Jim, "but I can't say that prison would be the answer. I imagine that Dr. Kim will advise putting him into a high security mental institution."

"My heart breaks for his poor mother," said Hattie,

"She loves him so, and now with her mother gone, she will be completely alone."

chapter forty

Dr. Kim sat on a chair in the den and faced Ronny. No one could have been less threatening, and Ronny, his recent anger spent, responded to him. Finally, Ronny took a chair, too. There was a pair of French doors in the back wall, and the doctor could see that they opened onto a flagstone patio. They were partly open, "Did you come in through those doors, Ronny?" he asked.

"The boy stared at them indifferently, "Yes, I did," he answered, "I didn't want to walk through the house and see those people."

"Once you were inside, then what happened?" asked the doctor.

"My mother was here," recounted Ronny, "She was crying. I hate crying."

"Yes?" prompted Dr. Kim.

"She told me about my grandmother's will. She told me that Grandma didn't leave me anything. Not anything!" He began to become agitated.

"That must have been very hard for you to hear," the doctor said sympathetically.

"Yes, it was," said Ronny, "My grandmother and I loved each other a lot. Why would she do that to me?"

"Perhaps it was a mistake," suggested Dr. Kim, "Maybe she died before she had a chance to finish her will." Ronny sat very still thinking about that possibility. Finally he said, "Yes, maybe that's what happened. She was going to leave me lots of stuff, but she died before she could write it in her will."

"Do you feel like telling me how your grandmother died, Ronny?," asked the doctor.

"I did it," he answered, "she cried a lot. She cried because Miss Farwell put all of those houses in the beautiful pasture. She used to say that Hattie Farwell ruined the view, and she cried some more.

"I tricked her into going into the garage apartment. Then she cried because I wouldn't let her out. She even banged on the windowsill with the high heeled shoes until I took them away and hid them under a loose floorboard."

"Then, what did you do?" asked Dr. Kim.

" I taped her mouth shut and taped her wrists together. I told her to stop crying. I told her I couldn't stand it! I kept her there a while. She kept on crying so I hit her and stabbed her in the chest with a knife I had. Then she stopped crying."

"Then what?"

"I wrapped her in a sheet and towels because she was bleeding. And I took her down to her car and shoved her into the trunk. Then I cleaned up as much blood as I could and buried the bloody clothes out in the back near the old gate."

"Did you look in her brown pocket book?"

"Yeah, I read some of the stuff, but it wasn't too important, so I put the pocketbook in the front seat of her car, drove her to Miss Temple's house, threw the pocketbook on a table with some others and opened the trunk of Miss Temple's car."

"How could you do that?" asked Dr. Kim.

"When I stabbed Miss Temple I took her pocketbook before I shoved her into the river. All her keys were in there, so I used them."

"Can you drive a car?" asked the doctor.

"Yes," said Ronny, "I drove my grandmother's body to Miss Temple's and put it into her trunk, and then I came home again. It was nighttime. No one saw me."

"Why did you kill Miss Temple?"

"She kept staring at me, and then she followed me. I had to stop her."

"You said you loved your grandmother and she loved you," said Dr. Kim.

"That's true," said Ronny, "But sometimes she got mad at me. Not much, though. Mostly she was very good to me, but she used to pick on my mother. Sometimes she yelled at my mother and bossed her around. I hated that."

"Did that make you angry?"

"Yes."

"Why did you go to the Red Hat Brunch?"

"In the market, Miss Temple told my grandma that the Red Hat Ladies were going to church and then to the Sunrise Bed and Breakfast for brunch. Miss Temple told my grandma that she was going, so I decided to go, too. I found my mom's purple suit in the garage and I bought a secondhand red hat at the store. The shoes were my mom's."

"What about the big dog, Wolf?" asked the doctor, "Do you still want him dead?"

"Yes," said Ronny, "I hate that dog, I really hate him!!"

"Why?"

"Because Miss Farwell loves him. Anyway I don't like animals.!"

"Did you tape his paws and mouth and beat him almost to

death and leave him by the side of the road to die?"

"Yes, yes I did. I hate him and I hate Miss Farwell. I wish he did die!" Dr. Kim looked steadily at the boy. He had an urge to brush his shaggy hair back from his eyes, but he didn't touch him. "Where did you get the brown uniform you wore as the process server?"

"In the top of the garage. It was probably the chauffeur's."

"The wire rimmed glasses, too?" asked Dr. Kim.

"Yep, and the Halloween make-up, too," said Ronny. It was apparent to the doctor that Ronny was becoming restless and disinterested in further conversation. Dr. Kim was beginning to question the accuracy of all of his statements, but he now knew what had happened. What Ronny had done.

"Ronny," he said, "Where did your mother go? Do you know?"

"She went back to the gardener's cottage," Ronny answered, "She probably went to bed. She's probably taking a nap."

"Will you be good enough to go get her, please?" asked Dr. Kim. Ronny spun around instantly and ran off through the French doors and across the patio in the direction of the gardener's cottage.

chapter forty-one

Hattie's phone rang. Jim rose from his chair at the table and walked over to the counter, "I hope you don't mind, Miss Hattie," he said as he lifted the receiver, "but it's probably for me." She smiled her assent and Jim spoke into the instrument. "Jim, this is Theodore Prime. Dr. Kim has finished interviewing Ronny."

"Good," said Jim, "What did he learn?"

"You won't like this, but I can't tell you. You will have to talk to Dr. Kim. He has sent Ronny down to the gardener's cottage to get Jayne, and he's now waiting in the den for her."

"He did what?" Jim exclaimed, "Are you telling me that he let that little murderer out loose?"

"Well, you might want to put it that way," Prime said.

"I'm on my way over right now!" Jim said, but before he could leave, the phone rang again. It was Forensics, "Lieutenant," said the specialist, "there was blood in the trunks of both cars. According to our tests, the blood is that of Alice Farnsworth. Also, the dirt on the Porsche matches that of the lawn on Miss Temple's property."

"Good," said Jim, "that's just what I thought. I'm going to the Wellington estate," he told everyone and ran out to his car. For a few moments the others sat around the table and said nothing. Finally Eileen spoke, "I'm sorry that I couldn't be more helpful," she said, "but please call me at any time if there is anything I can do." She got up and started for the door. Leigh followed her, "I'm disappointed, too," she sighed, "But call on me any time, too." Edie Rapp and the other Red Hatters picked up the extra copies of their pictures, thanked Hattie for her hospitality and left. Elaine stopped on her way out and lovingly stroked Wolf's head, "You get well soon," she whispered to the great dog. Hattie smiled warmly at her.

"You are blest with wonderful friends, Auntie Hattie," Walter said after they had all left. He strode to the counter next to the stove, "Does anyone want more coffee?"

"I do," said Hattie, "and I am not only blest with my friends, I'm also blest with wonderful relatives. She accepted a cup of coffee from Walter."

"Just a short time until Sunday," said Evelyn. "I truly hope that nothing happens between now and then to shake things up!"

"You can trust Jim," Benita said, "He's on top of things."

"Of course he is," said Hattie, but she was still concerned. At the Wellington estate Jim was disappointed that he could not question Ronny, nor would Dr. Kim disclose anything that he and Ronny had discussed, "Doctor Patient privilege I suppose," Jim said to Dr. Kim.

"Yes, Jim, I'm truly sorry," Dr. Kim answered.

"And I'm sure that the same Client Lawyer privilege still applies to you," Jim said to Theodore Prime.

"Yes, it does," Prime answered, "I will tell you this, though, Jayne came back to the house a while ago, but she refused to talk to Dr. Kim. She said she wanted to talk to Ronny first."

"I have my men digging on the grounds," Jim said, "And I have some further evidence on the crime, so I'll be back very soon." Before he left two of his men approached, "Glad you're here Lieutenant," one of them said, "We've found balled up bloody sheets and towels buried down near the back gate. There was a sharp butcher's knife with them. They are bagged and in our car."

"Good job!" said Jim, "I'm anxious to find out what Forensics will have to say."

chapter forty-two

On Sunday morning Hattie asked Walter if he would like to drive her car to church. She sat in the back seat and a very nervous Evelyn sat in the front next to her husband. As he had before, Walter went into the Sacristy to see Pastor Schmidt, but only for a few minutes. When he came out he joined Hattie, Evelyn, Jim and Benita in Hattie's usual pew. Terri had returned to Philadelphia. Before the service the pastor announced that the Parish Meeting would take place immediately following the service. "All members of the church are encouraged to attend," he said. When the service was over Walter handed Hattie her car keys and he, Evelyn, Jim and Benita rose and left the church. Hattie remained in her pew. Hattie watched them go and said a little prayer that all would go well for Walter and Evelyn. She hadn't been this nervous in about as long as she could remember. The meeting was called to order by President Jones of the consistory. Some business matters were voted on, and then it was time for the vote on a new assistant pastor. Before the vote, the president spoke glowingly of both Walter and Evelyn. Pastor Schmidt sat quietly off to the side, but Hattie had the distinct impression that he wanted to jump to his feet. Of course that would never do, she thought. Paper ballots were passed to the members of the congregation. "The ballots, as you can see, are marked with Walter Whyte's name with "yes" and "no" boxes beneath. Please select the box of your choice and put a check mark or an X in it and pass it back in." Hattie was becoming more nervous than ever. Walter said that if the vote were not unanimous he would not stay, she recalled, as she passed her ballot in. What if only one person votes "NO"? It would just break my heart... The ballots were all turned in, and then the tedious business of counting them began. Hattie's eyes were riveted to the secretary's hands as she unfolded each ballot, read it and placed it in a pile. One of the men counted them and wrote the results in a book. Hattie closed her eyes. When she opened them again the president was holding the book in his hand, "Ladies and Gentlemen," he began, "Trinity Church has a new assistant pastor! Can someone go out and find Walter and Evelyn? I want to congratulate them!" When Walter and Evelyn came back in the entire congregation stood up and applauded. Hattie and Evelyn both burst into happy tears. After the men of the congregation had congratulated Walter with hearty handshakes, and the women had hugged Evelyn, Hattie approached them and said, "Let's go back to my house for lunch and a little celebration." Jim and Benita joined them, and Benita produced a bottle of Chardonnay for a toast. "I have an offer to make," Hattie told Evelyn and Walter. "You don't have to give me an answer right away if you want to think about it."

"Please, don't keep us in suspense," said Walter, "What is it?"

"Do you want to call your parents first?" asked Hattie.

"No," said Walter. Hattie laughed, "OK," she agreed, "I love having you here, and I want you to move in permanently if you would want to live with me."

"Oh, Auntie Hattie," cried Evelyn, "that would be just wonderful."

"Yes, it would," Walter said, "We could both help you with things around the house, but we wouldn't be under foot. I think it would work out beautifully. Thank you ever so much!"

"Now we can call my parents!" Evelyn stated happily.

chapter forty-three

Hattie's heart sang when she woke up on Monday morning. She arose, bathed and dressed and descended her piecrust stairs as quietly as possible. Her joy at having Evelyn and Walter living with her made her want to dance. Wolf walked over to her, and she leaned over and hugged him, "Isn't it wonderful?" she said into his fur. She knew without doubt that there would be adjustments to be made in the new living arrangement, but she decided to take them as they came. Upstairs in their big back corner bedroom Walter and Evelyn were discussing the same thing.

"Do you think that Auntie Hattie will object to our moving our own bedroom furniture into this room?' Evelyn asked in some concern, "She's so generous that I don't want to do or say anything to upset her at all. I would like to fix up our portion of the house to suit us, but I don't want to step on her toes."

"Why don't we just wait for a while before we make any suggestions?" said Walter, "Anyway, we don't have any furniture yet. And since this is Monday, we clergy persons (ahem!) have the day off, so why don't we enjoy Auntie Hattie's company and relax a little?" When they had showered and dressed and gone down to the kitchen, they saw that Hattie had the coffee ready and was already eating a bowl of cereal, "Here," she said when she saw them, "Let me fix you some breakfast."

"No, thank you, Auntie," said Evelyn sweetly, "This is the first day of our new living arrangement, and I think we'd better discuss everything." She poured more coffee into Hattie's cup and filled two more cups. She gave one to Walter and took the other herself, "I don't want you to feel that you have to be our hostess any more. I want you to relax a bit."

"That's probably a good thing," said Hattie, "As you know I've lived here all by myself for many years, and I do think we should discuss the adjustments that you will have to make as well as my own."

"I love you, Auntie Hattie," said Evelyn.

"And I love you both very much," said Hattie, "I don't believe that we will have any trouble. There will be a few wrinkles to iron out, but we can do it! By the way, I have an appointment this morning in about an hour. I'll let you know when I'm leaving. I hope you won't need the car for a couple of hours."

"No," said Walter, "but that reminds me, Evelyn and I should be searching for a car of our own."

"Super!" said Evelyn, "What about Mrs. Farnsworth's Porsche?" Hattie and Walter both laughed, "Don't you think that would be a bit ostentatious?" Walter said with a smile.

chapter forty-four

Hattie's appointment was with Matt Borzio. She drove to Doylestown and was pleased to find a parking spot in front of his office. She was met in his waiting room by his assistant, Jo, who greeted her warmly and ushered her immediately into Matt's office.

"As you know," she said to him, "I am here to write my will." They sat down across from each other at his desk, and she began to state her wishes as he made notes. "I want to leave my house and three acres of ground to Walter and Evelyn. The remainder of my land is to remain protected in perpetuity. I also want my money to be divided equally between Nigel and Janice, their son, Justin, Evelyn and Walter and Jim and Benita Sawyer.

"Depending on how much money there is left, I want the church to have at least one thousand dollars. Also, as far as my things are concerned, I would love Terri to have some of my jewelry. I have a jade pendant which I think she would love. We'll have to discuss other things later."

"I'll start working on it right away, Miss Hattie," said Matt.

When she arrived home Hattie was humming to herself. She had been thinking of her will for some time, and now everything had fallen into place, "And that's pretty much that," she said aloud. But on the subject of wills, Jayne Farnsworth was still miserable. Once again she asked Theodore Prime if there hadn't been a mistake.

"No, not a mistake, really," he said, "but Dr. Kim suggested to Ronny that perhaps she had died before she had finished writing her will."

"Oh," said a somewhat mollified Jayne. Prime had accepted her invitation to take up residence in the mansion while the funeral was being planned. He also was anxious to keep her from becoming too upset about her mother's will. She came into the den through the French doors and sat in a brown leather chair from which he carefully brushed off plaster dust. She smiled at him, "Thank you," she said, "The workmen are almost finished now."

"If you agree," he said, "your mother's funeral will be held in the funeral home, and her body will be interred in the family mausoleum in Laurel Hill Cemetery on the East River Drive in Philadelphia. I've made all of the arrangements, but they can be changed if you do not approve."

"When?" she asked.

"Would Wednesday suit you?" he asked. When she agreed he went ahead with the plans. He knew that he should notify the papers, but he also knew that reporters were beginning to flock around all ready and an obituary could come later. Alice had no near relatives or friends here anyway. The police, of course, were in the midst of Alice's murder investigation as well as that of Meredith Temple, and he expected a news explosion at any moment.

"Jayne, I want you to remain out of sight here as much as possible. I also want you to keep the entrance gates closed at all times except for the police and Dr. Kim."

"What about Ronny?" she asked.

"Of course that goes for him, too," Prime said sternly, "He must not leave the estate either. Not for any reason. She said nothing, simply nodded her head.

chapter forty-five

By mid-morning Jim had rounded up one of the other officers and called James Sabath in Tinicum. "We have sufficient evidence against Ronny Farnsworth to bring him into headquarters," he said, "I believe that I should call Dr. Kim, though, before we go to the estate." He placed the call at once.

"I will meet you at the Wellington estate," said the doctor, "I believe it would be best. Also, I suggest that you call Theodore Prime. I think that he should know that you are coming. He's been staying in the mansion."

"Should I tell Jayne, too?" asked Jim, "Maybe she should be prepared."

"No," said Dr. Kim, "Mr. Prime will tell her if he wants to." Five officers left for the estate in two police cars, one car each from Plumstead and Tinicum. They drove quietly without lights or sirens. One of the officers swung open the iron gates, and both police cars entered the estate. No one was in sight. While three of the men walked around outside the mansion, James Sabath went with Jim to the gardener's cottage. The cottage was silent as they approached. They walked quietly onto the porch. Jim tapped gently on the front door, and there was no response. The door was unlocked, and they both drew their guns when they entered the living room. "Ronny," Jim called, "Are you here?" With their guns held out in front of them they searched the first floor, then cautiously ascended the stairs to the second. The bedrooms and bathroom were empty. They looked in the closets and even under the beds, but no one was there, as was the case with both crawl spaces. They then approached the mansion on the far side, away from the windows and French doors in the den in case Ronny was looking out. There was, however, no sign of him. When they tapped on the front door, Theodore Prime opened it at once. "Where is Ronny?" asked Jim, "We've searched the gardener's cottage, and he's not there." Prime looked alarmed, "Was Jayne there?" he asked.

"No," answered James, "the place was empty. We thought they would be up here." Dr. Kim came in during the agitated conversation between Theodore Prime and the officers. His face showed his concern but he said nothing. Right then two of the other officers entered the mansion with the news that they had searched the entire garage and had found nobody.

"Somehow," said Jim, "Ronny has found out that we were coming to arrest him. Search the grounds," he ordered his men, and he and James Sabath started to go out to join them. Prime stopped them, "I know that he did not go out through the front gates. I've been sitting here by the window since you called."

"I think," Dr. Kim said quietly, "that he left through the back gate. You had better hurry down to Miss Farwell's house."

chapter forty-six

Jim was suddenly gripped with fear, "Hurry," he ordered Sabath, "Let's get down to Miss Hattie's as fast as possible."

"Won't her niece and her husband be with her?" asked Sabath.

"This would be Walter's day off. I think they are going to look for a car," Jim said, "At least that's what they told Benita and me yesterday."

" They have probably borrowed Miss Hattie's car," he said when they pulled up in front of Hattie's house and saw that her car was not there. As they started toward the house they heard horrified screams and Wolf's deep growls. Then Hattie's voice rang out, ""Don't hit Wolf! Don't you dare hit Wolf again! Then Hattie cried out in pain.

"She's been hit!" Jim said as he crashed open the kitchen door. Hattie was lying on the floor and Wolf was standing protectively over her. Ronny was obviously in a rage and had a baseball bat over his head about to strike once more."

"This is for you, you damned son-of-a-bitch!" shouted

Ronny as he prepared to bring the bat down on Wolf.

"Try that and you are dead!" shouted James. He pointed his gun at the boy while Jim ran to Hattie's aid.

"I'm O.K., Jim, really," gasped Hattie, "I ducked when he swung the bat at me and lost my balance and fell down. I'm fine."

"Oh, what a relief!" said Jim. He hurried to handcuff Ronny's hands behind his back, but the boy fought so savagely that Chief Sabath had to help to subdue him. As they led the boy out of the house, Jim turned to Hattie, "Are you sure that you are really O.K.?"

"Don't worry, I'm fine, and so is Wolf." she replied. Once in the police car with the wire screen in place between the front and back seats, and Chief Sabath keeping an eye on Ronny in the back, Jim took a brief moment to call Benita and ask her to get over to Miss Hattie's right away. Then he notified headquarters that they had Ronny Farnsworth in custody and were on their way in with him.

chapter forty-seven

Theodore Prime and Dr. Kim pulled up in front of Hattie's house just after the police car left with Ronny. They both ran up the steps of the kitchen porch and knocked on the door. Wolf barked but did not menace the men when Hattie answered the door.

"Did Ronny come here?" asked Prime.

"He did, but the police drove him to headquarters just a while ago," Hattie told them. Both men thanked her and hurried down to their car. They were driving rapidly down the lane when Benita came in. "That car very nearly ran into me!" she said breathlessly when she rushed into the kitchen. "Who were they and what was their hurry? And what happened here? Jim called and told me to hurry on over." Ronny came here on his bicycle as usual" Hattie said, ."This time he was even more disturbed than ever. I have never seen anyone more possessed with anger than that boy. He had a baseball bat again, and he went after Wolf with it. I tried to stop him and he swung the bat at me. I ducked, lost my balance and fell onto the floor. Jim and Chief James Sabath came in right then. The chief had his gun drawn and threatened to shoot Ronny. Then they both grabbed him, put his arms behind his back, handcuffed him and drove him off in the back of the police car. Right after that Dr. Kim, the psychiatrist (you met him when he was staying at the Sunrise with his family), and Jayne's lawyer, Theodore Prime, came here looking for Ronny. They rushed off when I told them that the police had taken him to headquarters. That's all I know." Benita sat at the table and rested her face in her hands, "Miss Hattie, I am so glad that Evelyn and Walter are coming to live here with you. I know that you are more than capable of taking care of yourself, but you are so far away from everything, and things can happen."

"I cannot argue with you there," Hattie acknowledged, and they both laughed. In the police car, Ronny kept up a string of swear words, barely stopping for a breath as he did. Jim looked over at Chief Sabath and shook his head, "Have you ever heard a kid use such language as that?"

"Never," said the chief. At that moment the foul language ceased and they heard a fierce pounding on the window in the left side back door. James turned rapidly and saw Ronny lying on his back on the seat viciously kicking the window with both feet. Before Jim could stop the car, Ronny had forced the window loose and had pushed it out. Jim slammed on his brakes, but by the time both officers had jumped from the car, Ronny had maneuvered himself through the opening and had fled into the woods. "That kid sure has strong legs," James Sabath remarked as he started into the woods after Ronny.

"All that bike riding, I suspect," said Jim as he followed Sabath, "But how far can he run with his hands cuffed behind him?" Sabath suddenly stopped and leaned over to pick up a pair of handcuffs, "Well, I guess that's something we don't have to worry about!" he exclaimed, "Perhaps we should have taken Ronny's skinniness into consideration."

"There's no sign of Ronny anywhere," said Jim. Both men attempted to scan the woods, but there was too much undergrowth to see very far. "Let's get back to the car and call for back-up." They hurried back toward the road as rapidly as they could, but before they got there they heard a car start up. They crashed on through the undergrowth, but when they reached the place where Jim had stopped the police car it was gone. "Oh-mi-gosh," moaned Jim, "I left the keys in the ignition!" He used his portable radio to call headquarters for assistance. Fortunately, before he completed his call Theodore Prime and Dr. Kim pulled up, "What happened?" Mr. Prime asked, "Where's your police car, and where is Ronny?" He took a further look at their faces and added, "No, don't bother telling me. Somehow Ronny got hold of the car, right? Here, hop in, we'll take you wherever you want to go." As they started up the road, Dr. Kim said, "I believe that you will find your car back at the Wellington estate. I think that it is highly unlikely that Ronny would go anywhere else."

chapter forty-eight

Before they reached the gates of the estate they saw the police car parked in the circular drive. When they checked it out they found that it was undamaged. Jim immediately called headquarters for assistance. "Where would he be?" he asked Dr. Kim and Theodore Prime,

"We'll have to search for him."

"I don't believe that will be necessary," Dr. Kim said.

"Come into the house with us," said Mr. Prime, "We have some information for you." In the sitting room next to the den, they found Jayne sitting calmly apparently waiting for them. As usual she spoke politely to them when they greeted her. She looked neat and clean, dressed in beige slacks and a white shirt. On her feet she wore tan sandals. Her hair was brushed back from her face and she had on pale lipstick.

"Jayne," said Jim, "Can you tell us where Ronny is?"

"No, I'm sorry, I can't," she answered, "

"Jayne," said Mr. Prime, "Would you mind making us some tea?"

"I'll be glad to," she answered sweetly, and she left the

room.

"She can't tell you where Ronny is, because you see, there is no Ronny," said Dr. Kim, "Ronny does not exist."

"What?" said James, "But he does exist. We have all seen him."

"Yes, he even stole our police car," said Jim, "And on top of that he admitted killing Miss Temple and his grandmother, and he attacked Miss Farwell and her dog, Wolf, a number of times."

"That was Jayne," said Mr. Prime, "dressed like a boy. Like her son, Ronny."

"Jayne is very sick," said Dr. Kim, "She has what is known as multiple-personality disorder. She does not know it herself as far as I know, but I am going to have to examine her thoroughly. Unless I am very mistaken she has complete faith in Ronny's existence."

"But, but," Jim stammered, "Did Ronny ever exist?"

"Yes," said Mr. Prime, "But from what I learned from Alice, his grandmother, he was killed in a car accident when he was two-months-old. She wrote to me about it afterward. She blamed herself because she was holding the baby in her lap. Jayne was driving. Apparently a bee got into the car, Jayne swerved, and they ran head-on into another car. The baby hit the windshield and died almost instantly. Jayne was inconsolable. To her Ronny hadn't died. She kept his nursery as it had been until she thought he should move into a bigger room, and so it went until recently when she took on his persona. He would be 13 now going on 14.."

"You are her lawyer, Mr. Prime, as you know, we'll have to arrest her, but what then? She murdered two women including her own mother, but is she aware of that?"

"Probably not," said Dr. Kim, "But she will have to institutionalized. Fortunately there is a fine psychiatric institution outside Boston which I would recommend if the court agrees."

"Right now she will go to a local psychiatric hospital where she will receive excellent care," said Prime,

"In the meantime we'll talk to the District Attorney and the judge." Later that day the information about Jayne becoming Ronny was confirmed when Forensics reported to Jim that the finger prints at Hattie's house and in the gardener's cottage and the police car, believed to have been Ronny's, were actually Jayne's. Arrangements were made at once for her in the local psychiatric hospital. Jim drove her, but Dr. Kim and Theodore Prime went with her.

chapter forty-nine

Jayne was escorted to the psychiatrists' offices early the following day, "Hello, Dr. Kim," she said in her usual pleasant way, "They tell me you have some questions for me."

"Good morning, Jayne," Dr. Kim smiled at her, "I really want to help you get better, and I do have some things to ask you." She looked at him calmly and leaned back in her chair, "Yes?" she said.

"Let's go back a long time, O.K.?" She nodded at him,

"Tell me about when you were a little girl. Did you have a happy life with your mother and daddy?"

"He was not my daddy!" she exclaimed, "He was Anthony."

"Is that what you called him?"

"When I had to call him anything."

"How did you feel about Anthony?"

"I hated him!"

"Did you always hate him? Even when you were very young?"

"No. I started hating him on my tenth birthday. Really

hating him. I just didn't like him before that. It was servants' day off, a Thursday. My mommy had gone out for a cake or something. Anthony came into my bedroom, 'So, my pretty, we're all alone,' he said. He started touching me in my private place. He pushed me down on my bed and pulled my clothes off. I told him to stop. I yelled, 'Please stop!' but he didn't. He wouldn't let me up. Then he took off his pants, and he got on top of me, and he hurt me!" Afterward he told me that if I told my mommy he would say I was a liar. He even said he would kill my kitten!"

"Did he ever do it again?"

"All the time! Every chance he got he came into my room and did it. He even did it when I grew up, but then I was used to it and I just let him. But all the time I hated him more and more!"

"Jayne, can you tell me if Anthony was Ronny's father?"

"Yes, he was. And when he found out I was pregnant he ordered me to have an abortion. I refused and he hit me, but I would not have an abortion. Then my chance came. He had planned a hunting trip in the mountains with some of his friends. We had a lodge up there, and I drove up when they were going out in the woods. I followed them and I shot him. No one knew. They all thought it was an accident. They thought it was a poacher who shot him. I was a good shot, and it was Anthony who taught me how to shoot. Isn't that ironic?"

"Do you want to tell me about Ronny?"

"He was a beautiful baby. I cannot describe how I loved him. How much he meant to me. Then one day my mother and I went out in the car with Ronny. She held him in her lap, and I told her to put him in the car seat. She said 'we aren't going far,' and she held him. I was driving. Suddenly a bee came in through my window and started buzzing around my face. I tried to swat it away and lost control of the car. We smashed into another car. Ronny was thrown into the windshield. My mother said he was dead, but I knew he wasn't. That's why I tore up her diary. Fourteen years of lies about Ronny! Ronny is not dead!"

Jane was obviously upset, but she remained outwardly calm. The doctor realized that Jayne could never release the rage within her. Rage against her step-father, against her mother and even guilt and terrible anger against herself. So she allowed Ronny to show all of the rage that was bottled up inside her."

chapter fifty

That evening Hattie overcame the objections of Evelyn and prepared a roast turkey for dinner. The only people there were her favorites, Evelyn and Walter and Benita and Jim. Benita insisted on making the gravy and mashed potatoes while Evelyn made coleslaw and stuffing.

"This is the first time I have ever made American stuffing," she announced. The talk around the dinner table centered on Jayne and the shock to all of them when Jim made the startling announcement that there was no Ronny. "How weird!" said Benita, "I wouldn't have guessed in a million years that Ronny was really a 49-year-old woman!"

"Do you believe that Ronny will show up again?" Evelyn asked.

"I don't know," said Jim, "but if he does he will not be able to get out of the hospital. Of course, his clothes won't be there, either. I don't know enough about Jayne's illness to make any kind of prediction, but I'm certain that she will never be released unless she is completely cured. Dr. Kim will be keeping a close eye on her, but it doesn't seem possible that an individual who has murdered three people would ever be let loose on society again."

"Did she show any signs of viciousness when you saw her?" asked Walter.

"No, that was the spooky part. She was very charming and sweet, too. You would never have believed that there was anything wrong with her. You all would have liked her," Jim said.

"Was she aware of the fact that she had killed Meredith Temple and her own mother?" asked Hattie.

"No, I believe that she thought that she was completely innocent. I truly believe that she had no idea what Ronny did when he appeared," Jim said.

"Surely, though, she must have known that she shot her step-father to death," said Walter.

"Yes she did, but in her mind she was justified. You see he had been molesting her since she was 10-years-old. And then he tried to make her abort her baby when he discovered that she was carrying his child." Jim said.

"Oh, how sad," said Benita, "does anyone know this? Did Alice know? It seems strange to think that Alice wasn't even suspicious."

"That's something that we'll never know," said Jim.

"Alice's funeral will be on Wednesday at the funeral home," said Hattie, "I can't imagine that there will be anybody there. Would any of you want to go with me?"

"Of course, I will," said Evelyn and Benita said that she would go, too."

"Thank you both", said Hattie, "I hope that will be the last funeral we'll be going to in a long time." Over a dessert of ice cream and cookies, Hattie said,

"And now a complete change of subject," She left the room for a brief time and came back with a large paper bag in her hands, "This," she said, "is my way of saying that there is a very pleasant time ahead." She opened the bag and produced a beautiful red felt hat, decorated with ribbons and flowers, which she immediately placed on her head.

"Now on to the future!"